In memory of Freda Deary
November 21, 1913—March 14, 2005
Thanks, Mum.

KINGFISHER
a Houghton Mifflin Company imprint
222 Berkeley Street
Boston, Massachusetts 02116
www.houghtonmifflinbooks.com

First published in paperback in 2007
2 4 6 8 10 9 7 5 3 1

LIBRARY OF CONGRESS CATALOGING–IN–PUBLICATION DATA
has been applied for.

ISBN 978-0-7534-6118-1

Printed in India

1TR/1206/THOM/SC/60BNP/C

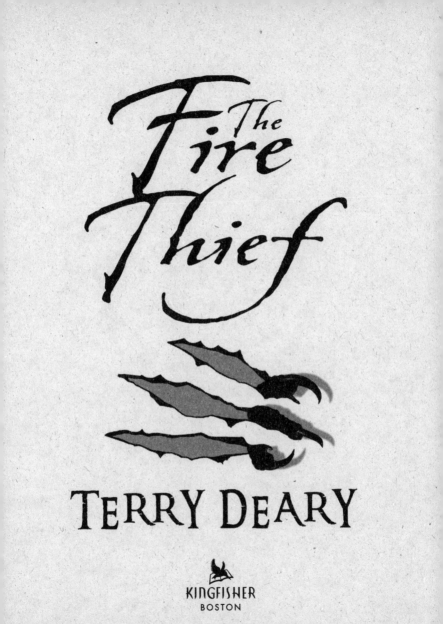

The Fire Thief

TERRY DEARY

KINGFISHER

BOSTON

ONE

GREECE—THE DAWN OF TIME

This is where my story begins. I wasn't there myself in ancient Greece, but one of the actors in this terrible tale told me the story, and I believe him. Let me tell you his story as if I was a writer—I've always wanted to be a writer. Who am I? Wait and see. Let's start at the dawn of time . . .[1]

The bird soared and wheeled in the cloudless sky over the silent earth. Beneath it lay valleys of rich green and white-topped mountains. A crystal blue sea shone in the distance. A deep forest loomed beneath

---

1 Yes, all right, maybe not the exact dawn of time. Not the first hour of the first day. But one million years ago, when humans were nothing more than very clever apes. Some of them still are. But now we call them police officers. Heh! Heh!

the monstrous bird, and from the heart of the darkness a smudge of smoke rose into the clean air.

"Ahh!" the bird growled. "Fire." It scented the sooty air and climbed away from it. Then it turned and arrowed toward a distant mountain. "Breakfast," it hissed, and then it swooped down. Rabbits froze, terrified as the bird's death shadow passed over them. The bird ignored them and let the warm air lift it up the mountainside.

As it climbed, the shimmering grass below gave way to gray, wind-scrubbed shrubs and then bare rocks, too bleak for even moss to grow.

The bird lifted its hooked beak and half closed its curved wings till it dropped toward one massive boulder. On the boulder lay a man. Windburned and sunbaked, he lay there as the bird's claws clattered against his rock and it skidded to a halt. "Oooops!" the bird croaked. "After all this time I'm still not good at landing."

Fine chains had sunk into the rocks, and they wrapped around the man's wrists and ankles. Fine links—but unbreakable.

The bird shook its gold-brown feathers, and its black eyes burned. "Good morning, Prometheus.

I hope you slept well," the bird hissed.

The man smiled. His face was as handsome as a god. "I slept very well."[2]

The bird blinked. "You seem cheerful," it snapped suspiciously.

"I slept well," the man cried. "And had such wonderful dreams! I dreamed of freedom."

"You don't deserve it," the bird snarled. "You stole fire from the gods, and you gave it to those crawling creatures they call humans. You sneaked it away, hidden inside a reed—you are no better than some robber on the road." The bird began to screech and ruffle its feathers. "The humans will burn our world and choke us all with smoke. You deserve worse than death . . . Fire Thief."

Prometheus smiled again. "And I have a punishment worse than death, don't I? My cousin Zeus chained me here in the sun and snow, in the wind and hail, always to suffer but never to die."

A big gray tongue rolled from the side of the bird's

---

2 Our characters spoke in ancient Greek, you know. But you would not understand it, so I have changed it into our language. I am being very kind to you, so stop complaining about the realism and keep reading. Trust me, I am a liar.

cruel beak. "And worse, Prometheus, and worse. You have me. The Fury. The great Avenger of the gods." The bird began to pant. "What am I going to do, Prometheus?"

Prometheus opened his eyes as wide as a baby. "Oh! I don't know! What have you done every day for the last two hundred years, Fury? You have used your little beak to peck into my side and pull out my liver. You have killed me every morning for one hundred years. And every night I return to life to suffer again the next dawn."

"I don't peck," the bird snarled. "I *tear*."

"Feels like a peck to me," Prometheus said with a sad shake of his head.

The Fury was furious. "I don't pull your liver—I *rip* and *rive* it from your body."

"Feels like a little tug to me," the man shrugged, and the chains rattled against the rock.

The bird's claws clattered as it stamped angrily. "I wish Zeus would let me tear out your lying tongue and your laughing eyes," it screeched.

"Sorry, just my little old liver," the man sighed. "Come closer, Fury."

The bird froze. "What?"

"I want to tell you about my dream."

"Why would I want to hear your dream? You'll be dreaming the dreams of the dead in a moment when I *tear* and *rip* your body."

"Ah, it was such a dream, though. The sort of a dream you have once in two hundred years," the man murmured.

The bird edged closer. It wiped its beak against the cold rock to sharpen the tip. "Lift your head, Prometheus," the bird screeched. "Look at the valley. That smoke down there choked me this morning. Smoke from the fires that YOU gave to those pitiful human animals. Your liver will taste all the better this morning."

The bird lunged at the man's side. The hand of Prometheus slipped free of the chain and grasped the bird by the neck. It gave a startled squawk. Its black eyes bulged, and its body struggled. But the more its body writhed, the more its neck ached.

"I haven't finished telling you about my dream," the man said, and his voice was as soft as his hand was hard. "In my dream my friend Hercules came up the mountain. He is the strongest creature in the world. Stronger than me." Prometheus sighed and squeezed the feathered neck a little harder. "Stronger than you. And Hercules snapped my chains like they were made out of grass. Just like I am going to snap your neck now."

The bird writhed and croaked. "You said it was a dream."

"I lied," Prometheus said with a laugh. "I still have friends." He squeezed again. "Strong friends, like Hercules. Good friends who think that I was unfairly treated. Friends who sent Hercules to set me free last night."

"A dream, you said!"

"A dream come true."

"Zeus will never let you escape," the bird gasped. "No matter where you try to hide on this earth, he will find you."

Prometheus shrugged and shook off the broken chains. "Maybe I won't hide in this world," he murmured. He squeezed. There was a crunch of broken bone, a small sigh, and the monstrous bird hung limp in the man's hands. He flung it away from him in disgust, its cruel beak and curved claws clattering on the cool rock.[3]

Prometheus rose and stretched. The world lay

beneath him. He set off down the mountainside, his legs stiff from 200 years of chains.

He felt like he was being watched. He stopped and looked back. The eyes of the monstrous bird were dull and dead.

He squinted up into the morning sun and saw a shadow cross it. The shadow of a long-necked bird. A swan.

The young man closed his eyes for a moment and groaned. "Zeus," he hissed. "Zeus." He looked for somewhere to hide. But on the bleak, bare mountain there was nowhere at all.

3 Look, please don't cry or sigh for this monstrous bird. And do not write letters complaining about cruelty to animals. First of all, this was an avenging devil—you wouldn't want to meet one of those in the bathroom, believe me. It was only taking the shape of a bird. And, anyway, you don't know what happened next—just wait and see.

TWO

EDEN CITY—THE YEAR WE CALLED 1858

Now the story switches to my childhood. This part really did happen. I know because I was there, wasn't I? If this jump of one million years confuses you, then you must have a very small brain. Stop reading and start knitting or whittling sticks. If you are NOT easily confused, then keep reading. Go ON. What are you waiting for?

I'll never forget the week my uncle Edward died. Well, to be honest, he died twice. And that was odd because most weeks he only died once.

And that night he had some trouble dying the *first* time, and he blamed me. He always did!

We'd arrived in Eden City—the darkest, dankest, dreariest city in the world. It was also the most wicked and watchful.

The crooked streets were made for strangers to get lost in. It was almost as if the city *wanted* you to get lost. A wide lane tempted you to travel that way—but, when you did, it twisted and then turned and then led you to a wide, wooden wall that there was no way past. You turned and found that there were two ways back—and whichever path you chose would be the wrong one. Then, when you walked into another wide wall, you heard a soft snicker. You turned. There was no one there. It was the sly city itself that was laughing at you.

We didn't know that when we left the station. We asked a match girl, "What's the way to the Storm Inn?"

She pointed a frozen finger along the misty street. "Go straight ahead till you come to the crossroad, and then turn left toward the river."

But there is no "straight ahead" in Eden City, just a tangle of turnings—bleak back alleys that never see daylight. Little lanes that seem to head the way you want to go but lead you into someone's yard where pecking chickens and petrified dogs fall under your feet.

Eden City was a shapeless swamp that sucked you

in. It must have mystified mapmakers. Some buildings were made out of strong stone, and some were smoke-black brick—most were wobbling wood that reached up till their tops were lost in the thick air—but all had windows that looked out like blind eyes.

The people in the street walked past with eyes just as empty and faces just as hard as the cold cobbles.

If you ever wanted to make your nightmares come alive, then Eden City was the place to go. So why did Uncle Edward take us there, you ask?

Because no one knew us there, I answer. If they had known who we were, they may have locked us up or thrown us out—or worse.

We smelled the rat smell of the river and turned toward it. Suddenly, we stumbled on the Storm Inn. That soft snicker again. Eden City had tormented us for long enough—like a cruel cat playing with a mouse—and now it set us free and dropped us at the door that we'd been looking for.

"It is fate, my boy," Uncle Edward said. "We were meant to find this happy hostelry." It wasn't fate—it was Eden City letting us loose because it knew that worse was waiting for us.

"It looks like a happy pigpen," I muttered. But we

went in and took a room.

We left our cases and our coffin and slept with cockroaches for company.

The next afternoon we set out for the richest house in Eden City. This time we took a clattering cab that rocked and rattled us over cobbles. Somehow the cab horse found its way through the drifting fog and only got lost twice. We paid the silent and scowling driver—he scowled because Uncle Edward didn't give him a tip. Uncle Edward never tipped.

The house stood at the end of a curving drive. Stone steps led up to a door as wide as a barn with a brass knocker as wide as my head . . . though my head in those days was not very wide.

Uncle Edward brushed the afternoon mist off his faded black jacket and set his yellow cravat straight. He rubbed his scuffed shoes against his gray, checked pants and was ready.

He knocked.

"We are strolling players," Uncle Edward told the butler. "We entertain with our little show."

The butler was carved from ice. "Go to the Storm Inn—they do shows with vagabonds like you," he said, and I swear that icicles dripped from his tongue.

Uncle Edward reached into his pocket and swept out a scroll of parchment. My uncle did everything with a sweep. He unrolled it—with a sweep—and swept it in front of the knife-sharp nose of the butler with a sweep.[4]

"A letter from the mayor of this gracious city," Uncle Edward said. "The mayor is an old, old friend. We went to school together." As the butler reached for the letter, Uncle Edward swept it away.[5] "It says . . ." He cleared his throat and read the scrawl. "'This is to introduce my good friend Mr. Edward Slaughter, actor, musician, and star of the world's finest stages. This brilliant man will entertain and educate your friends and guests with his magnificent masterpiece, "The Uncle." What is more, there is no charge for this awesome art. (Your guests may care to reward him with riches if they feel Mr. Slaughter has brought riches into their lives.) Signed, His worship the Mayor of Eden City.'"

4 Look here, can I stop all of this sweeping now? You must get the picture. Every time Uncle Edward does something, just think to yourself, "With a sweep." If you will do that one small thing for me, I will get on with the story.

5 Oops! Sorry!

Uncle Edward bowed.

"You're lying. What's his name?" the black-suited butler barked.

"Whose name?"

"The mayor, of course, his name?"

"Why . . . Mayor. I always call him Mister Mayor."

The butler shook his head. I swear I heard his neck bone creak. "You went to school with him."

"I did?"

"You *said* you did."

"Ah, yes, we were boys together . . . at least I was," Uncle Edward laughed.

"So, what did you call him at school?" the butler snarled.

"Which school?" Uncle Edward replied.

"Which school? The school you went to with the mayor, of course. Which school was it?"

"Don't you know?" my uncle gasped.

"Why, no."

"So? How do you know I didn't go to school with him?"

"Because you don't know his name!"

"Neither do you," Uncle Edward smiled.

"I do," the butler growled, and spots of anger burned on his ghost-white cheeks.

"You don't!"

"I do!"

"So what is it?"

"Mayor Walter Tweed!" the butler said, and he almost smiled.

"Well done!" my uncle cheered. "You DO know little Wally's name."

"You call him Wally?" The stone-faced butler's stone face cracked in shock.

"We called him Wally when we went to school," my uncle chuckled.

"Of course."

"And good old Wal sent us around here. He said your master would be pleased to see us. He has a party every Friday night."

"He does." The butler nodded. "All rich folks have parties on Friday nights."

Uncle Edward hopped up to the top step. "You ARE his butler, aren't you?"

"Of course." The stone-faced frown was shocked and even shaken.

"So? What's his name?"

"His name?"

"Your master's name!" my uncle wheedled.

"It's Mucklethrift . . . Master George Mucklethrift," the butler babbled.

"Correct!" my uncle cheered. He turned to me. I stood on the bottom step shivering in my thin-soled shoes. Soles as thin as rainwater. Soles as thin as my weed-thin arms and legs. "Jim!" he said.[6] "Jim, we've met an honest man. It's rare to meet an honest man these days." He peered into the face of the butler. "Do you know the last time I saw an honest man?" he asked softly.

"Why, no!"

"When I looked in a mirror," Uncle Edward lied. "Let's go inside and look around."

"Around?" the butler gasped.

"Why, yes! We need to look around." My uncle shrugged his shoulders so wide that they wobbled.

"You're a stranger," the guardian of the door said.

Uncle Edward hauled himself to the top step. "And you were a stranger to me till two minutes ago. But I trust you, don't I?"

---

6 He called me Jim. That could be my name for all I know. He took me from the orphanage when I was only six years old. My name at the orphanage was Six-four-two. Uncle Edward called me Jim. I called him Uncle—even though he wasn't. I hope you followed that. You did? *(cont.)*

"I suppose so."

"So let's start our new friendship with a little trust. We need to see your drawing room—the room where we will do our show tonight."

The butler bowed his creaking head. He couldn't help himself. "Come in, Mr. Slaughter."

"Call me Edward," my uncle said and used his arm to guide the butler through the door—into the warmth and golden light. With his free hand, my uncle waved to me to follow. Fingers of fog followed us in as if they were the city's spies keeping the city's eyes on us.

I knew my job. While those two looked around the drawing room, I would explore the house and seek out all the riches.

After all, we weren't there to do our show and collect pathetic pennies from the rich. Oh, no. We were there for a whole nother reason . . . [7]

6 *(cont.)* Now get back to the story. I am shivering on the step, so hurry up, please.

7 It can be really annoying when a writer stops a story just as it is getting interesting. It makes you keep reading when you really should be shutting off the light and going to sleep. Writers should not be allowed to do this. But writers DO do this. And I want to be a writer, so I will do it too. Complain all you want. This is MY story, and I will tell it as a writer would. Sorry . . . Why did I say that? I'm not *really* sorry.

THREE

GREECE—THE DAWN OF TIME (BUT FIVE MINUTES LATER)

You may remember that we left Prometheus—one million years before my time—walking down the mountain. Free at last. You may also remember that he was spotted by a passing swan. He knew that the swan was Zeus in disguise. Then, just when you were wondering what happens next, I stopped the story of Prometheus to tell you my story. You don't have to wonder any longer. Here's what happened next . . .

The swan swooped and landed in front of Prometheus. You could see by the sag in the young man's shoulders that he was sickened by the sight of the swan. It was a look that spelled "defeat."[8]

The young man had lived 200 years, chained to that rock, having his liver torn from his body every single morning. He had smiled and even laughed through that hideous pain.[9] But now he was in despair. "Hello, cousin," he sighed.

The swan shimmered in the sunlight, and beneath the feathers you could see the shape of the god Zeus. "Hello, Prometheus. Going somewhere?"

The young man tried his liver-losing smile. "Just for a little walk."

"Ah." Zeus nodded and threw off the swan wings. "I hate walking. Hate it. I prefer to fly myself."

Prometheus looked bitter. "Just a pity you were flying past the mountain this morning and caught me," he said quietly. In fact, it was so quiet that you could have heard the butterfly that flapped past the god and his cousin.

8   Which is better than a look that spelled "defeet" or "difeat" or even "diffeet." If you are going to have a look that spells anything, then make sure it can spell correctly. Nothing worse than a look that spells rongly.

9   Yes, I know that if he'd been chained there 200 years, he must have been around 220 years old. So we can't call him a "young" man. But he died every morning and was born again every night. So, really, he was never more than one day old, was he? We could call him "baby," not young man. Ha! You never thought of that, did you?

Zeus shook his head. "You don't understand, Theus. When you killed the Avenger, the Fury, it didn't just die without a trace. It sent a spark into the sky that showed me that it was dead. We gods may die—but we always go out with a brilliant spark. Don't you know that?"

Prometheus shook his head. "I'm a Titan—only half god," he said. "Maybe I don't have that power."

"But you do, cousin. Every morning when you die, you give out a brilliant spark. I watch for it from Mount Olympus, you know," the great god explained.

Theus screwed up his face, puzzled. "You saw one of those dying sparks this morning when the Fury died. How did you know that it wasn't me?"

Zeus's face was brilliant and beautiful, as bright as the sun and so large that it seemed to fill the gaze of Prometheus. It was almost a human face—a human face that looked pleased with itself. "When a god dies, it goes out with a golden spark—when a human dies, it goes out with a miserable blue light."

"And me?"

"Half and half, my cousin. Mix blue and yellow, and what do you get?"

"Purple?"

Zeus sighed. "One day those pitiful human creatures will invent a torment for their young. They will call it a 'school.' They will trap lots of their youngsters into a small room and force them to learn facts."

"How cruel!" Theus cried. "If they fail, will they have their livers ripped out?"

"Worse," Zeus roared. "They will be told that they are worthless and will be made to feel useless. They will be seen as failures. They will have to live their lives with the scorn of their friends. They will be given new names."

"Names?"

"Names like Dunce and Dolt, Clod and Chump, Nitwit and Numskull, Fool and Fathead." [10]

"Those words hurt," Theus said. "But why are you telling me this?"

"Because you are Prometheus the pieface, Theus the twerp. One day those school brats will be taught

---

10 He could have added Oaf, Nincompoop, Ignoramus, Ninny, Bonehead, Pinhead, and Blockhead—they were just a few of the names that I suffered in the orphanage. Those words hurt more than the beatings by bullies and the sly pinches, more even than the cruel canings of the teachers. Zeus was right. It is amazing how a god could look into the future and see the savagery of schools.

that yellow and blue make green! Even the dumbest dunce will know that. Your spark is green. You are half god and half human. You didn't know that gold and blue make green? Maybe I should send you into the future in the shape of a little child and make you go to school. Maybe I should make you suffer the cruelty of the classroom," Zeus said slyly.

The young man's eyes widened. "No, cousin, no. Send me back to the rock. Let me have my liver ripped out—my heart, my lungs, my eyes, my tongue—twice a day . . . but don't make me go to one of those school places." [11]

Zeus tilted his handsome head to one side. "Theus, you are a rash and foolish Titan . . ."

"A dunce and a dolt," Theus agreed.

"You took fire from the gods, and you gave it to those humans. Look down to the valley . . ."

Prometheus turned his head and looked over the gray-green slopes to the woods below. Amber flames

---

11 Of course, we are all afraid of things that we've never seen. You are probably like me and afraid of the bogeyman that lives under your bed. Bogeymen are scary because you've never seen one. You just know that yours is there. And Theus was scared of school because he'd never seen one. Zeus made schools sound scary. You've been to one. You know the truth—they are not a little bit scary—they are much, *much* worse than that.

leaped from a clearing, and humans ran like ants to feed their fires with torn tree trunks and broken branches. A breeze caught the rising smoke and sent it curling toward his nose. He sniffed. He coughed.

"That is just the start," Zeus said. "One day their world will be filled with their flames and choked with their smoke. Birds will fall from the sky because the air will be poisoned with those fumes. Earth will be smothered by a blanket of fog that will hold in the heat and melt the iciest wastes. The planet will flood and drown. And it's all your fault, Theus. Why did you give them fire?"

Theus spread his hands. "They are such clever creatures, and I love them. Titans, gods, and humans—we are all made from the dust of ancient stars. We are all cousins."

"I don't want humans for cousins," Zeus said sourly.

"The gods gave the beasts fur and the birds feathers. But they left the humans unfinished. So the poor hairless things had to huddle in cold caves. I gave them fire to warm them."

Zeus frowned, and a thundercloud rumbled over his head. The cloud grew bigger and grayer till it blotted out the sun. There was a flicker of lightning, and rain fell from the cloud till it soaked the human fires in the valley. Steam hissed from the charred wood and made rainbows in the air. Zeus roared, and the land shook. The humans ran and hid in the forest. "The gods are the heroes!" Zeus cried. "We are the great ones. We rule the world! These humans are vermin—worse than the rats and the snakes and the locusts that we scattered on Earth to tease them."

"Humans can be heroes too," Prometheus argued.

Zeus blinked. The clouds began to clear, and the sun shone through. "Humans can't be heroes. You can search till the end of time and not find me one human hero," the god spat.

"Give me a chance," Theus said.

Zeus laughed. "A chance? A challenge? I like that, my cousin. A little fun. Life can get boring on Olympus, you know. I may just grant your wish . . . give you a chance."

The god laughed, and the humble humans in the valley below trembled—the laugh sounded like the howl of a mighty, man-munching monster. They feared that they would be its breakfast.

FOUR

EDEN CITY—1858 AGAIN, SAME EVENING

Just as Prometheus had talked his way out of a return to his chains, so Uncle Edward had talked his way into the house of Mr. George Mucklethrift. For some reason, I keep wanting to call him George Muckletwit. That would be a rude thing to do. I may be a crook, a thief, and a liar, but I am usually very polite. I really am. Don't argue with me, dimwit.

After the dark, dank streets of Eden City, Mr. Mucklethrift's house was so warm and bright that I felt like I had walked into Aladdin's cave. The butler made me take off my scuffed shoes and stand inside the door while he took Uncle Edward into the drawing room.

Uncle Edward would go over every inch of that

room, arrange the seating and the lighting, check the piano—and even the piano stool. It would take him ten minutes. No more, no less.

A tall clock ticked in the hallway. I jumped as it began to chime five o'clock. I had to be back here by ten past five with a list of the best things to steal. Not large things—lots of small but precious things. As many as we could cram into a coffin.[12]

The hall had tables with ornaments and paintings that we could rip out and roll up. But the paintings were all too new. Mr. George Mucklethrift was not one of those people from an old family. His money was new.

The biggest painting showed a tweedy man in a weed suit . . . or do I mean a weedy man in a tweed suit? Whatever, the man in the painting had a fat gold chain around his skinny neck. Mr. Mucklethrift kept a painting of Mayor Walter Tweed in his hall. What a creep. The mayor must have been a guest, I guessed. Maybe he'd be there this evening. But I didn't have time to stand and stare at paintings—unless they were

12 Yes, that's an odd thing to say. Why a "coffin"? Why not a sack or a suitcase, a pocket or a purse, a big brown box or a bigger, browner barge? Wait and see.

valuable paintings.

Five rooms opened off the hall. They were warmed by coal fires, and that made me shiver. All that coal made tons of soot. And skinny boys like me were pushed up chimneys to sweep it out. A master chimney sweep with black fingernails almost took me from the orphanage to climb the cramped chimneys of the rich. Uncle Edward offered more money and got me instead.[13]

There were mantel clocks and golden cigar boxes, candlesticks, dishes, and silverware—knives, forks, spoons—little picture frames with grinning girls, black-hatted men, and well-washed women. There was fine china by the cartload—no use to us. Throwing it into the coffin would chip and crack and crush it all. As Uncle Edward said, "You can't melt china."

The first time he said that I was only six years old and ignorant. I answered, "No, Uncle. You can't melt Japan or India or Africa either."

13 Yes, I know you think I'm a villain—robbing from the rich. But it's better than choking in those rich folks' chimneys. If I was caught, I knew that I'd choke on the end of a rope instead. But that would be better than swallowing black dust till I died. Somehow getting myself hung seemed like a clean end.

He sighed and explained. "We steal gold and silver, and we melt it down. We sell the metal, not the ornaments or spoons. That way no one knows where it comes from."

"So, when we go to China, we don't try to melt the country, Uncle?" I was very young and slightly simple, as I said.

Uncle Edward shook his head. "When I say 'china,' I mean 'china'—cups and plates and platters and bowls. It's what we drink from."

I nodded happily. "Tin cups and plates. I know."

He rolled his eyes. "Jim, in the orphanage you would drink from tin cups and eat off tin plates. Outside the orphanage most folks eat from china—not the country, the pottery."

"Potty?"

"Pott-e-ry," he said.

"What's pottery?"

"It's clay. Clay that has been baked hard."

"Clay is mud!" I cried. "The rich folks eat from mud? I'm glad I'm not rich then, Uncle."

That was when he walked away muttering something about selling me to the chimney sweep.

But I learned fast, and I had a good memory. In

Mucklethrift Manor I knew just what we could take from those rich rooms.

I raced upstairs. Mr. Mucklethrift and his rich guests were in most of the rooms—I could see the gaslight spilling out from under the doors and could hear the people moving. But a bathroom was empty, and there were silver combs and hairbrushes, soap dishes, and ivory-handled razors.

Time was ticking and tocking away. I opened the bathroom door. Maids were scurrying along the landing, laden with clothes to dress the elegant people. Every time a servant slipped into a room, another one would come out from another door. Time ticked on. Uncle Edward and the butler would be back at the front door, and I'd be missing. The butler would call for a search, and my spying trip would be discovered.

Tick, tock, tick, tock, tick—knock.

Knock?

A knock at the front door.

Just at that moment the landing was empty. I jumped onto the sweeping banister and flung myself into a swift slide. I hit the hall floor just as the drawing room door opened and the butler stepped out. He looked down his icicle nose at me, crumpled on the floor. He was about to say something when the knock came at the door again. The butler crossed the hall to open it.

Uncle Edward stood in the doorway of the drawing room and frowned at me. He looked out as the front door swung open.

In the glare of a gaslight stood a man. A tall, thin man with a mustache as thin as a shoelace. He was wearing a uniform with a bright badge and brighter buttons. His cap had a smaller badge.

"Good evening, Sergeant Sergeant," the butler said. "What can I do for you?"

The policeman leaned forward, and his chicken neck stretched out. "I've come to warn you that there is a cunning pair of thieves in the area."

I glanced across at Uncle Edward. Thin strings of fog seemed to slide past the policeman and wrap themselves around Uncle Edward's collar. He closed his eyes and held his throat. He could already feel the rope tighten around it.

Oh, dear.

Oh, dear.

Oh, dear, oh, dear, oh, dear.

FIVE

GREECE—THE DAWN OF TIME HAS ROLLED ON
TO THE MORNING OF TIME

*Would you believe it? Just as we have stepped into the arms
of our imprisoner, Theus is stepping free from his. There is a
saying, "Where there's life, there's hope." So Theus has hope
every day. Even chained to a rock for all of eternity, he has
hope. But for us at that moment, in the passageway of
Mucklethrift Manor, we had no hope. That's life—or I
should say, that's death. But you don't want to hear about
my problems. You probably have enough of your own. Hear
instead about the good news of Prometheus . . .*

Zeus sat on the rock and rubbed Prometheus's chains
between his hands. They crumbled to dust. His
mighty finger pointed to the edge of the woods.

"I vowed that you would be chained to the Caucasus Mountains forever," he said. "I cannot break my vow."

Prometheus looked gloomily at the rock.

Zeus gave his crafty look again. He picked up one of the links of the chain and squeezed it till it made a circle. Then he took a small piece of the mountain rock and rested it on the link. He breathed out fire to weld the rock onto the link. There was a smell of burning flesh—Zeus had scorched his finger.

"By Cronus, this fire is even too dangerous for a god," he murmured and sucked on his burned finger. Then he took the link with the rock and slipped it onto the finger of Prometheus.

"What is this?" the Titan asked.

"I think I will call it a 'ring.' With this ring, you are still chained to the mountain rock yet are free to move around. I vowed that you would be chained to the rock forever—and as long as you wear the ring, you are!"

"Thank you, cousin," Prometheus said quietly.

A hairy little human was stepping out from the dripping trees and had picked up a sharp stick. A horse was grazing on the plains. The human was crawling through the grass so that he could get close enough to kill it.

"See that, Theus?"

"Yes, cousin. He is hunting to stay alive."

The god gave a nod. A sort of god nod.

"Just like you, my boy. You are the hunter. You will go out and try to find one good man who makes all of the other creeping creatures worth saving."

"A hero?"

"A hero. You are the hunter." Zeus leaned forward and suddenly pointed to the edge of the forest. A silver shape slipped through the trees and stopped. It fixed its glittering eyes on the back of the hairy human hunter. "See that, Theus?"

"A wolf—it is hunting the human!"

"That's right, Theus. The hunter doesn't know that he is being hunted."

You wouldn't want to know what happened next . . .

You would?

Oh, very well. The hairy human reached the hairier horse and raised his spear. The horse saw the human and snapped at him in fear of the spear. He chewed the stone tip off the spear, and it was useless—not a spear any longer, just a stick with a frayed end.

The man was furious. "That stone tip was a gift from my mom!" he cried. The man jumped forward in a fury and wrestled the horse to the ground. (It was no bigger than a pony.) He tried to force the pony's jaws open as he shouted, "Give me my gift back, miserable horse! Give me my gift."

He was so busy wrestling with the pony that he didn't see the wolf till it was too late. The wolf sprang and with its fangs tore at the hairy human. The pony galloped off.

Zeus laughed. "You see? Beware, Theus. While you are hunting, make sure some hunter doesn't catch *you*."

"But you will give me a chance, cousin, won't you?"

"I will," Zeus promised. He reached down and swept up the swan wings. "Here, Theus. Put these on. Rise above Earth. The higher you go, the faster Earth will spin. The more it spins, the more time will pass. You can go to any point in time . . ."

"And I can go to any place in this world?"

"Of course. Search it and find yourself a hero. Do that, and the gods may forgive you."

Theus grinned a joyful grin. "I will, cousin." He spread the wings and felt the air begin to lift him. "I'll find one truly great man or woman—one true hero."

He rose into the air. Zeus had to shout. "There are just three things before you go . . . "

Prometheus was rising faster than a bubble in a boiling pot.

"First, I cannot call off the Fury—wherever you go, the Avenger will be searching for you . . . As you hunt, you will be hunted—and next time it may destroy you completely. You will be trying to escape from the Avenger forever, unless you find a hero first." Zeus picked up a link of the chain and crushed it into dust between his fingers. "The Fury may turn you into powder and scatter you to the wind—you will be returned to the dust of ancient stars and die forever."

Prometheus looked down at the shrinking figure of his cousin and at the gray-green-blue-brown patchwork of Earth. "The Fury is dead!"

Zeus shook his head. "So were you at this time yesterday. But you came back to life."

Prometheus looked at where the big bird lay. He thought he saw its golden feathers stir. It could have been the soft wind ruffling them. Then it turned its broken neck stiffly and seemed to half open its evil eye. Prometheus let himself drift down a little and was sure that he heard the monster bird's crackling voice creak one word: "Revenge."

Prometheus beat down strongly with his arms and climbed above the highest clouds. He was so high that he could see Earth begin to turn beneath him. "What was the second thing, cousin?"

Zeus called up, "You must never cheat—you must act like a human. Never use your godly powers!"

"I don't have the same godly powers as you," Prometheus answered.

"You have the power to die and come back to life. But remember, when you die, you give off a green spark—no other creature shows a green spark. It will betray you to the Fury, and you will be ground into a powder."

"I understand," the young man shouted and let the wind carry him higher. "What was the third thing?"

Zeus looked up in horror and pain. "Before you go, take me home to Mount Olympus! I hate walking. Absolutely *hate* it!"

But it was too late. Prometheus was sailing past the Moon and watching Earth spin ever faster. Days passed, then weeks, then years. One thousand years.

Cold planets whirled around him, and hot suns hissed past. Stars drifted through black space in clouds like diamond dust, whizzing and spinning till little Earth vanished like a grain of sand on a beach. One million years had slipped away.

He was safe out there—safe from the tearing beak of the Fury. Safe—but lonely and bleak . . . Prometheus missed the comical creatures that they called humans. He had to see them again, even if it cost him his freedom or his life.

He closed his wings and drifted down.

One million years, he guessed, had passed. Of all the planets that whirled like grains of sand in a storm, he scented Earth like a dog scents a single sausage in a garbage can.

The Fury would never find him now—at least not before he'd finished his quest and found himself a human hero.

Just to be sure, he headed for the shadowed side of Earth, 10,000 miles away from Greece.

SIX

EDEN CITY—THE HALL OF MUCKLETHRIFT MANOR

We left my story with the policeman just about to catch us in the act . . . at least getting ready to do the dreadful deed. You say, "There is no way out! Jim and Uncle Edward will hang—it serves evil Edward right. But poor little Jim doesn't deserve to die." (At least I HOPE you are saying that.) "Will Jim escape? Or is he writing this from a prison cell? I simply MUST read on."[14]

---

14 Leaving the reader in this state is called a "cliff-hanger." At least that's what writers call it, and I want to be a writer. Of course, I didn't leave us hanging over the edge of a cliff, but we may as well have been. So go on, turn the page. But please don't lick your finger before you do. It is a bad habit, and it will ruin the book. On the other hand, you may have just used your finger to pick your nose. In that case, please DO lick your finger before you turn the page.

"There are two tricksters going around," the policeman said. His eyes were gooseberry pale and twice as large. His mustache trembled. He read from a notebook. "A fat old man and a skinny boy," he went on.

Uncle Edward spluttered and covered his mouth with his blue-spotted handkerchief. I swear he was going to say, "I am NOT fat!" Instead he stepped from the shadow of the drawing room door into the candlelit hall.

The policeman was reading from his notes. "They worm their way into a rich house and put on a show. While the fat old man talks to the guests, the skinny boy robs the house. They robbed a house in Baker Flats and were seen getting on a train headed for Eden City."

"Aha!" Uncle Edward cried. The butler turned. The policeman blinked. "Aha!" Uncle Edward said again. "I have heard of these two villains. They have robbed houses in Denville and Borchester, Diddlehampton, and Quigley, too!"

The policeman peered at his notebook. "They have!" he said.

"And you say they are headed for Eden City, Officer?"

"Sergeant."

"Sorry, Sergeant. Sergeant what?"

"Sergeant."

"I heard you . . . Sergeant what?"

"Sergeant Sergeant."

"Sergeant Sergeant what?"

"Just Sergeant Sergeant," the policeman said.

Uncle Edward shook his head. "You say they are headed for Eden City, Sergeant Sergeant?"

"They are! And they have a coffin . . ."

Uncle Edward crossed the hall, and the policeman's notebook was in his hand before the sergeant could move. My uncle peered at the page. "Fat old man? Wrong! Wrong! Wrong!" he moaned.

"Wrong?" the butler asked.

"Wrong?" the policeman echoed.

Uncle Edward looked up to the ceiling—it was his "tragic" look. His bottom lip trembled as if he was about to cry. His voice became a high and pitiful whine, swooping to a low sob. Uncle Edward was acting. "I . . . have seen these cruel criminals."

"You have?" the policeman gasped. He looked over his shoulder into the dark street. The butler pulled him into the hallway and slammed the door. They put their backs to the door.

"In Denville," Uncle Edward moaned.

"Phew-w-w!" the policeman and the butler sighed.

"They robbed me . . ." Uncle Edward's voice was breaking. "They robbed me of my most precious watch. The old gold watch that my grandfather gave me when he was a child!"

"When *you* were a child, Uncle," I piped up.

He glared at me. "As little Jim says . . . when *I* was a child." Suddenly, he wailed, "They robbed me of my watch! Ahh! The pain." He reached into his vest pocket and pulled out a gold watch that we'd stolen in Mango Creek. "This watch! This very watch that I loved with all my heart," he sobbed.[15]

"We watched them do a show—well disguised," Uncle Edward went on. "The *thin young* man stuffed his waist with pillows to look . . . plump. And the skinny boy was . . . was . . ."

"A skinny girl, Uncle," I said.

15 Yes, that's right. You've spotted Uncle Edward's mistake. Why didn't the policeman notice it? Because Uncle Edward was such an amazing actor. A fat old fraud—but a great actor. If only you could have heard him. If only someone could invent a machine to show moving, talking pictures. But, impossible, I know.

"Yes! Excellent, Jim. A *girl*! You are looking for a young man and a *girl*," Uncle Edward sighed.

The policeman reached for his notebook. Uncle Edward quickly ripped out a page and said, "That's all wrong . . . all wrong."

Sergeant Sergeant said, "It says here something about a coffin being part of the trick . . ."

My uncle's hand shot out faster than a grasshopper's leap and snatched back the book. "Ah! No! Ahh! Ha! Yes! But no!" he choked and tried to chuckle. "We saw the act, didn't we, Jim?"

"Yes, Uncle."

"And there was no coffin, was there, Jim?"

"Yes, Uncle."

"What!?!"

"There was a lot of coughing. The fat old man couldn't stop coughing. When the people rushed to help him, the skinny boy slipped out of the room and robbed the house," I explained.

"Exactly!" Uncle Edward breathed again. "The *thin young* man couldn't stop coughing. When the people rushed to help him, the skinny *girl* slipped out of the room and robbed the house. See?" he said, tapping the notebook. "Not coffin—*coughing!* You are the victim of a spelling mistake." He ripped out the page and stuffed it into his pocket.

Sergeant Sergeant shook his head in wonder. "So you would know this thin young man and the girl if you saw them again, would you?"

"Oh, yes. Once seen, never forgotten," Uncle Edward roared. "And I will squeeze my grandfather's watch from the fat-thin hand of that old-young rogue."

The butler bowed his stiff neck. "Perhaps, Mr. Slaughter, as you will be here tonight, you can keep an eye out for them."

"I'll say," Uncle Edward said. "I'll keep two eyes out . . . no, *four!*"

"Four?"

"Me and little Jim."

"Of course."

The butler opened the door and let in twisting ropes of mist—twisting like the rope that would hang us when we got caught. "Then I look forward to seeing you at six-thirty—your performance will begin at seven, before Mr. Mucklethrift's guests have dinner."

Uncle Edward bowed in return. He slapped the

notebook back into the hand of the gooseberry-eyed policeman and stepped out into the mizzling mist. I slipped back into my grubby shoes and followed.

The door closed. Only the distant flare of a gas streetlamp lit our way down the drive. Uncle Edward strutted toward the road. Water dripped like a ticking watch onto the gravel at our feet and then ... stopped. The city was listening. "I thought I did very well there, Jim. Watch me and learn. One day you can be a master like me. Well? Did you seek out the most robbable riches?"

"We can't go back tonight," I said flatly.

"They suspect nothing!" he cried. "My performance was masterful."

"There's a picture of Mayor Walter Tweed on the wall."

"So?"

"So—if he's a friend of Mr. Mucklethrift, he will probably be there tonight."

"So? So? Your point, boy? What are you trying to say?"

"You showed the butler a letter from Mayor Tweed. It said that he knew you. It said, 'This is to introduce my good friend Mr. Edward Slaughter.' But you're *not* his good friend. He *doesn't* know you. And when you get there this evening, you'll be found out."

Uncle Edward sucked damp air through his teeth and blew out a cloud of breath into the cold night. "Let's worry about that later, why don't we? Another problem for another day."

"But . . ." I tried to object.

Uncle Edward was striding out down the road.

I could feel the ropes tighten around our necks. [16]

16 "Aha!" you are saying to yourself. "Those two will NOT hang. If they did, then how would he be here now, telling the story?" Maybe I am in the prison cell right now, waiting to go to my execution. You didn't think of that, did you? That's because you're not a writer like me—or at least like I hope to be.

SEVEN

TEN MILES ABOVE EDEN CITY—1858

This is a very unlikely setting, I know. People can't fly even one mile above a city. People can't fly—period. They can hover up there in a hot-air balloon, I suppose, but humans will never be able to fly, will they? You have to remember, though, we have gone back to Prometheus, and he has the wings of Zeus to help him. Now you'll see how the two stories start to come together—but not completely together. Yet.

"Oh, Zeus, what have I done?" Prometheus whispered as he hovered over Eden City. "I gave the humans fire, and now the world is in flames."

Looking down, the young man could see a cloud of purple and yellow, green and brown, gray and black. It hung over the evening city like a stained rag over a maggoty lump of rotten meat. Twisting towers and sharp spires rose out of the mists to meet him. The city looked like a dirty mattress with nails pointing up to the sky.

But there was something worse. The nails seemed to be reaching up for him. Clutching claws. His liver ached. The city reminded him of his enemy, the Fury. Theus rose upward again, wary and watchful. Was Eden City hiding the Avenger? Or were the city and the eagle partners in grime?

Over on the sunset side of Earth, Theus could see mountains and forests, rivers and plains, as clean and green as they were back in Greece. His aching arms wanted to carry him to the cool lakes and the cream wheat fields to the west. He sighed. "If I'm to blame for this evil air, then I suppose I have to go to the heart of it."

He dropped toward the dead air of Eden City.

As he dropped down to the tips of the towers, he was swallowed by the damp and stinking smoke. It stung his eyes—the tears and the fog blinded him for a while.

Lower.

A string of lights—the pale green glimmer of gaslight alongside the mud-splattered streets. The yellow glow of oil lamps and candles behind grimy windows. Blue lamps by the busy police stations. And one bright red lamp outside a tavern door, behind a red glass sign that said "Storm Inn." The wooden inn wallowed on the waterfront. Barges bobbed in the greasy water and grated against the dockside.

Prometheus swooped over the deck of a barge and landed in the road outside the inn. Splash.

No one saw him land. [17]

There was a snort and a hiss and a rattle as a carriage rushed toward him. "Get out of the way, you idiot!" the cab man shouted. Prometheus leaped out of the way, and the carriage splattered him with mud as the driver cursed. "Just stand in the road if you want

17 I suppose you'll think that this is strange. Some big Greek myth floats down on swan wings over a crowded city, and no one sees him? "Of course not," you cry. Well, I was in Eden City in 1858. You looked at the ground so you didn't step in a mud-filled hole—you looked into the shadows so some cutthroat didn't leap out to grab you—you looked over your shoulder to see if you were being pursued by some pickpocket who was after your wallet. But, believe me, you did not look up in the air for flying myths. That's why they mythed him . . . missed him . . . mythed him. Get it? Oh, never mind.

to be knocked over, you great big ninny!"

The young man wanted to ask, "Is a ninny like a dunce or a dolt, a clod or a chump, a nitwit or a numskull, a fool or a fathead? And am I in a 'school'?" But the driver was swishing away into the shadowy distance.

Prometheus slipped the wings off his back and stepped carefully between the puddles onto the wooden sidewalk in front of the inn. It was early evening, so it was quiet inside. But one man in a drab jacket sat at a beer-soaked table and sipped his drink.

There were swinging doors at the front of the inn. Prometheus peered inside. He watched, amazed, as a man with a thick gray beard rubbed a pink-tipped piece of wood onto the side of a box. Fire sprang to the tip of the little stick. Then the man put a wooden tube with a little bowl on the end into his mouth—he stuck the flaming stick into the bowl and sucked on the tube.

"No!" Prometheus gasped. "I didn't give you fire so that you could drink it!"

But the man sat back in the creaking chair and looked content. Prometheus wandered in through the swinging doors. He stepped onto the stained sawdust that covered the floor. The man with the pipe looked him up and down. The smoker saw a young man dressed in nothing more than a thin tunic and sandals. "Good evening," he said with a nod. "Cold?"

"Not as cold as a winter night on the mountain," Prometheus said.

The man with the pipe shook his head. "I mean, are you not cold at all—wandering around like that without any pants on?"

"Pants?" Prometheus understood the word but not the idea. [18]

The man with the pipe waved a leg covered in gray material. "You know. Pants, trousers . . . drumstick cases. They keep your legs warm and your unmentionables covered."

"Unmentionables?" Prometheus looked down at his legs and lifted up his tunic. Like all ancient Greeks,

18 "Aha," you say. How did Prometheus understand the English language? Full of questions, aren't you? Well, I'll tell you. Being half god, it was one of his powers—he could read your thoughts, the pictures in your mind, not your words. See? Simple. Now can I get on with the story, please? I don't know about you, but I want to find out what happened next.

he wore no underclothes.

The man with the beard choked on his beer. "Here! Cover yourself up."

"Why?"

"Because they'll lock you away, that's why."

"I've been locked away two hundred years," Prometheus said sadly and dropped his tunic back in place.

"Huh?" the man asked.

At that moment the door behind the bar clattered open, and a girl hurried in. She was a skinny thing with hair that would have been red if she'd washed it. It hung in rattails around her ugly face.[19]

"Here, January," the man with the pipe said. "This young man has no pants. Just came out of prison— locked away for two hundred days, he says. They must have stolen his clothes while he was inside."

19 This girl, you will see, is January Storm, the innkeeper's daughter. She has read my story and tried to change parts—she can be very bossy and thinks she knows better than a writer (like me) how to write a book. She wants me to say that she was not really ugly. She says she has a "hidden inner beauty"—all I can say is that it's very well hidden inside of her. She has a face that would scare a dragon. Oh, and her hair isn't red, she says. It's "auburn." Yeah—and so is my tongue.

January Storm put her leather bucket down. "You look like you're the same size as Big Bill," she said and dived behind the counter. She came back up with a bundle—a shirt and a black suit. "You can have them."

"Won't Bill want them?" Prometheus asked.

"Not where he's gone," January cackled.

"Where's he gone?"

"The graveyard. He dropped down dead last night."

"That's sad."

"It was—he hadn't paid for his food and drinks. We took his clothes to sell. But they're not worth much—you can have them!"

"You are kind," Prometheus said. "Can I repay you?"

January looked at him brightly and picked up her leather bucket. "Yes, you can scatter this fresh sawdust on the floor before we get busy, and then you can wipe down the tables and sweep the stage."

"Stage?"

"The platform over there—we have some dancers on tonight." She placed a hand over her mouth and gasped. "Oh! You're not with the dancers, are you?"

The man with the pipe piped up, "I told you—he's just come out of jail."

"No-o," January said. "He's got those fancy wings tucked under his arm. I thought they might be for the dancers. I mean, a big guy like him isn't going to go around fluttering his wings like a fairy, is he?"

"No," the man with the pipe agreed. "So what are the wings for if you aren't a dancer?"

"So that I can fly," Prometheus said.

January looked at the man with the pipe. The man with the pipe looked back at her. Prometheus saw the look and knew what it meant. "You think I'm a ninny, don't you?"

January looked at him gently. "I think you need to get dressed in Big Bill's clothes, and I think I need to give you a good meal."

"A meal?"

"You'll love it—made it fresh myself," she said proudly.

"What have you cooked tonight, January?" the man with the pipe asked.

January smiled her yellow-toothed smile and poked Prometheus. "You'll love it," she promised. "It's a nice tasty piece . . . of *liver*!" she said.

"Oh, no," Prometheus groaned, and he fainted onto the soggy sawdust.

At that moment the doors swung open, and in walked . . .

EIGHT

THE STORM INN, EDEN CITY

At last, the two halves of our story come together. "And it's about time!" that ugly reader with a face like a potato says. Well, let me tell you, potato face, everything comes to him who waits—or her who waits . . . or it that waits. Whatever. If you haven't guessed who walked through those swinging doors, you haven't been paying attention.

Uncle Edward and I stepped through the door of the Storm Inn and saw a curious sight.

A man with a beard sat at a table with a spluttering pipe in his mouth and a glass of beer in front of him. Nothing odd there.

The ugly, auburn girl (with inner beauty and rattailed hair) stood with a bucket of sawdust in her hand. Nothing odd there either.

A man lay on the floor in the beer-soaked, bloodstained sawdust.[20] He was tall and handsome, although his hair was a little too long. He had muscles like a cart horse. Nothing odd there. But he was dressed in a white tunic, and a pair of swan-feather wings lay by his side.

I think *that's* a little odd, don't you?

"He fainted," the girl said.

I put my hand over my mouth in shock. "Oh, no! Don't tell me that he saw your face without the bucket over your head!" I cried.

There is an old Greek legend about a woman named Medusa. She had snakes instead of hair. One glance from her could turn you into stone. That's just what January Storm looked like at that moment. "I offered him some dinner," she spat.

I covered my eyes with my hands in horror. "Ahh!

20   Didn't I mention the bloodstains? There were a lot of fights at the Storm Inn. They didn't bother to mop up the blood or sweep up the stained sawdust. They just scattered clean sawdust on top of it. Do you know that the Romans did the same sort of thing in their blood-soaked arenas? Gladiators bled and died—servants scattered fresh sand over the gory pools, and they kept on fighting. Uncle Edward told me that. I wish he hadn't.

The poor man! The thought of your cooking is enough to make any man sick."

I had only known January for one day, but already we had learned to loathe one another. "Please turn your bad breath the other way," she snarled. "It's burning my hair."

"The last time I saw something with hair like that it was eating a banana," I said with a smile.

"You're so ugly that you just walk in a room, and the mirrors run and hide!"

"Children! Children!" Uncle Edward shouted. "Enough! We have a sick young man here. Let's see if we can help him." He reached over to the table and picked up the beer. He poured it over the young man's face.

The man with the beard wailed, "That's my beer! Cost me good money, that beer did. What am I going to drink?"

"Uncle probably saved your life," I muttered. "The Storm Inn beer is probably poison if it's as foul as that bar girl."

January was about to say something spiteful when the young man moaned softly. He stirred and looked around. "Good evening, sir," Uncle Edward said, sweeping off his hat with a sweep.[21] "Edward Slaughter, actor, comedian, tragedian, and poet, at your service."

"I'm Prometheus," the young man said, sitting up.

"A fine and ancient name," Uncle Edward said. "The name of a Greek god, if I am not mistaken."

"Half god, half human," the young man said. "A Titan, actually."

"Uncle Edward is an expert on Greek legends," I said.

"My friends call me Theus," he said. "I don't want to use the name Prometheus here—I don't want my hunter to track me down."

"He has just come out of prison," January explained. "Served two hundred days for his evil crimes. They robbed him of everything when he left jail. Even his clothes. We were just going to dress him in Big Bill's clothes," she said.

"Poor Bill," Uncle Edward sighed.

"Poor Bill," I agreed. "He died after eating your stew last night, didn't he?" I asked.

---

21 Did I mention that he did everything with a sweep? I did? Oh, sorry. I'm still new to this writing stuff, so I am bound to make a mistake or ten.

"He died because he got into a fight outside," January said.

I shrugged. "All I am saying is that it's odd—he ate your stew and died soon after. You're not a cook—you're an assassin."

January's face turned as red as her hair and almost as dirty. "And all I am saying is how would you like this bucket of sawdust smacked around your ears?" I stepped back.

She stepped forward. "I could hardly miss those ears, could I? You could swat flies with those ears."

"There are plenty of flies in here to swat," I teased.

"Why don't you put your teeth in backward and bite yourself," she said and raised the bucket.

"Be silent, you pea-brained, chump-headed children!" Uncle Edward ordered. "I will lock you in a closet together and throw away the key."

"Ugh!" January said with a curl of her nose. It's what they call a Roman nose—it's roamin' all over her face.

"Ugh," I agreed. But I fell silent.

"Now, January, I will take young Theus up to our room and dress him in Big Bill's clothes. Jim and I will get ourselves ready for this evening's show . . . Put the young man's wings under the stage. We'll pick up our coffin from there later."

Theus struggled to his feet. "I promised to help Miss January with the cleaning—I need to repay her for the suit."

Uncle Edward shook his head. "Don't worry about that, my boy. I have a job for a jailbird like you . . ."

"I'm not really a bird," Theus said. "I borrowed those wings from my cousin."

Uncle Edward waved his words aside. "I need a strong boy like you to do a little carrying. Are you with us?"

Theus bowed his head. "I am honored to be of help," he said.

"But first we have to dress you properly. Hurry— we don't have a lot of time."

"We don't start the show till eleven o'clock," January said. "You've got plenty of time."

"Ahh! We have the honor of doing a show for Mr. George Mucklethrift this evening. We will return after the show and entertain your guests," he promised.[22]

---

22 We had to entertain the Storm Inn crowd to pay for our room, of course. Otherwise we would've gotten out of town with the Mucklethrift loot as soon as we could. Maybe we should have done that, and all that trouble with the hanging wouldn't have happened . . .

He led Theus to the stairs and climbed up to our room above. (The cockroaches would just have to make room for big Theus, poor things.)

January Storm gave a huge sigh. "Oh, my." *Sigh*. "My, oh, my!" *Sigh, oh, sigh*! I've always wanted to see inside a house like Mucklethrift Manor," she drooled.

"Take me with you," she said to me.

"We're working," I said. "Doing a show," I added . . . though our real work was robbery, as you know.

"You could take me with you."

"Take you with us?"

"Like a date—you could take me out."

"Ha!" I sneered. "Even the tide wouldn't take *you* out."

I was pleased to have had the last word. I turned my back. Big mistake. A moment later a sawdust bucket flattened my ear into my skull.

Ouch.

NINE

THE STORM INN, EDEN CITY—LATER

A writer needs to learn a little bit about "pace." So let's jump forward a few minutes. You don't want to hear about what happened after January Storm smashed my head with a sawdust bucket—how I tried to tear her red hair out by the roots and was pulled off by Uncle Edward and Theus. You don't want to know how we climbed up the dark stairs to our room. Let's just get there, why don't we?

I sat on the bed and played "Race the Cockroach" while Uncle Edward helped Theus get dressed in Big Bill's clothes. From time to time I rubbed my sore ear and cursed the ugly girl downstairs.

Big Bill must have been a sharp dresser. The black suit was almost clean, the shirt was almost white, and

Uncle Edward fastened on one of his own starched collars. The vest was decorated with silver threads, and there was a black hat that made Theus look like a gambler.

As Theus stuffed his arms into the sleeves, a few playing cards fell to the floor. They were an ace of clubs and an ace of hearts. "How did they get there?" Theus asked.

Uncle Edward spread his hands. "Big Bill was a card shark. I think he cheated some fellows out of a lot of money last night. They were waiting for him in the alley at the back of the Storm Inn. They planned to give him a beating and get their money back."

"A beating?" Theus asked as he tried to scrape spots of blood off the front of the shirt.

"He died, the foolish man," Uncle Edward said. "It served him right."

"Served him right? For cheating at cards?" Theus asked.

"No—served him right for having such a thin skull. Never be a card shark if you have a thin skull," Uncle Edward said and wagged a fat finger in Theus's face.

Theus frowned. "I'll remember that, Mr.

Slaughter." He straightened his clothes and looked in the mirror. He looked as if he'd never worn pants and a jacket before.[23] He walked up and down the room in his black boots and crunched cockroaches under his soles till he got used to the feel of the clothes. No matter how long he wore them, he would never look right—and the cockroaches never looked right either after Theus had walked all over them.

"What do you want me to do for you, Mr. Slaughter?" he asked as he looked in the mirror and played with his thin necktie.

Uncle Edward looked sly. I knew he didn't want to tell Theus too much—after all, if he had said, "We're off to rob a house of all its gold and silver," then Theus may have wanted a share.

Or Theus may have been a police spy. Instead Uncle Edward told half the truth. He waved a hand at me. "Little Jim and I are actors. We perform anywhere that there is an audience. I am but a poor player that

---

23   All right, YOU know that he'd never worn pants before—you've seen the pictures of Greek gods floating around in creamy, dreamy robes. But I didn't know then what I know now—that Prometheus wasn't just any old Prometheus. He was THE Prometheus.

struts and frets his hour upon the stage and then is heard no more."[24]

"You want *me* to strut and fret?" Theus asked, looking worried. "How do I do that?"

"That's just a saying. Shakespeare," Uncle Edward said.

"You want me to shake a spear?"

"Shakespeare was a writer—dead many years, alas."

"Did he have a thin skull too?" Theus wondered.

"Shakespeare. Great writer."

"Why did the writer shake a spear?" Theus asked.

"No . . ." Uncle Edward was getting irritated. "I see that you've never been to school!"

Theus looked afraid. "No, but I've heard about them. Cruel places where children are made to look like fools . . . where they're called names like Dunce and Dolt, Clod and Chump, Nitwit and Numskull,

24   That was a silly thing to do. Of all the plays that Shakespeare wrote, there is one that is cursed. You should never recite lines from that play when you are in a theater, or bad luck will strike you. Now, the Storm Inn wasn't exactly a theater, but it was where we would do our show later that night. The "strut and fret" lines are from the play that I am too afraid to even name, or it would curse this book. We actors call it "The Scottish Play." Did we have bad luck that night after Uncle Edward spouted those lines? What do you think?

Fool and Fathead."

Uncle Edward had been sitting on the bed. He rose to his feet and rested a hand on Theus's shoulder. He looked him in the eye, though he wasn't tall enough. So he looked him in the top button of his shirt. "Theus, my boy, all I want *you* to do is help us carry a box."

"A box? I can carry a box."

"Good. Little Jim and I usually struggle to carry it to our shows. Little Jim is a frail child—barely strong enough to tie his own shoelaces."

"No, I'm not, Uncle," I cried.

"Jim is so weak that he couldn't pull a greasy stick out of an elephant's trunk."

"I could!" I argued.

"You could?"

"I could!"

"That's good."

"That's good? Why is that good?"

"Because," Uncle Edward said with a glimmer in his eye, "you can carry one end of the coffin, and Theus can carry the other."

"What will you be carrying?" I asked.

"I, dear Jim, have to carry the worries of the world

upon my broad shoulders. And I will carry the magic lantern," he explained.

I sniffed. I'd been tricked and cheated—again.

"What is this coffin?" Theus asked.

"Ah," Uncle Edward said. "It is not a real coffin—it is a piece of stage furniture. What we actors call a 'prop.' We need it when we do the famous poem called 'The Uncle'—you will see it tonight at the Mucklethrift Manor show," he promised. "Then, when the show's finished, you can carry it back here and hide it."

"Hide it? Why?" Theus asked with a puzzled frown.

"Ah, um . . . because people don't like to see coffins lying around. It reminds them of their dead friends and loved ones. A coffin upsets people . . . so get it back here, as fast as you can, and hide it under the stage."

Theus snapped his fingers . . . and another playing card fell out of his sleeve. The ace of hearts. "I can bring it back and leave it on top of the stage," he said and looked pleased with himself.

Uncle Edward narrowed his eyes. "Why would you want to do that, my boy?"

"Because you are doing a show at eleven for the people at the Storm Inn!" he said. "You'll need the box on stage for that show."

"No!" Uncle Edward said sharply. "For that show we will do a different story. We will do the story 'The Boy Stood on the Burning Deck.'"

"Why did he do that?" Theus asked.

"Because, my boy, he was a hero. You'll see." Uncle Edward began to tell the story of the boy who stood on the burning deck, but Theus wasn't listening. Theus had a dreamy look in his eyes and was murmuring to himself, "A hero . . . yes, that's what I want to find. A hero. Then I can go home."

But Theus was a long way from home and a short way from a very tight noose . . .

TEN

GREECE—THE DAY AFTER THE DAWN OF TIME

"How annoying," you say. "That writer said the two stories were coming together. Now he toddles off back to Greece. That writer lied to me. I am upset." Don't be. While we were planning our robbery of Mucklethrift Manor, there were things happening in another time and another place. Things that will affect my story. So, even though I wasn't there, I can piece together the sort of thing that went on.

Zeus sat on his throne with his feet in a bowl of warm, salty water and made a face that would frighten a phantom. "Ooooh! My feet hurt! I hate walking. Did I ever tell you that I hate walking?"

"Yes, dear," his wife, Hera, said and poured more

water into the bowl.

"I walked all the way from the Caucasus Mountains."

"Serves you right for giving your wings to cousin Prometheus," she sniffed.

A monstrous eagle squatted on the side of the throne. Its neck had a strange twist to it, as if it had been broken . . . which, of course, it had. "Yes, serves you right," the bird growled.

Zeus patted the head of the Fury. "Yes, yes."

The Fury was angry—it was Furious. "Stop that patting. I'm not some pet parrot, you know. I am the most fearsome Avenger in the world."

"You don't look so fearsome now that you have that funny little twist in your neck," Hera said sweetly. It made the Fury furiouser.

"When I catch Prometheus again, I'll tear more than his liver. I'll tear his ugly head off; I'll rip his legs off; I'll eat his eyes . . ."

"Yes, yes," Zeus sighed. "But you'll never find him. He's flown. Gone."

The bird's feathers fluttered in the breeze. "I will find him if I have to search all over Earth."

Zeus's feet hurt—it's a long way from the Caucasus

to Olympus. That's why he said a stupid thing—he was thinking about his feet and not watching his tongue. "Yes, but you can't search till the end of *time*."

The bird turned its neck slowly and stiffly—because it was stiff.

"What did you say?"

Zeus dabbled his feet in the water and made a pained face. "Nothing."

"Time? Prometheus has escaped into another time?"

"I didn't say that," Zeus said quickly.

"Big mouth," Hera muttered.

But the bird was shuffling its claws on the marble floors in excitement. "It makes sense. Prometheus couldn't hide from me in this world. He would have to move through time—my guess is that he'd move into the future . . . thousands of years into the future . . ."

"At least," Zeus muttered miserably. Hera threw up her eyes to the heavens.[25]

---

25   There's a saying, "Threw up her eyes to the heavens." But, of course, Hera was already IN the heavens . . . because she was a goddess. So to throw her eyes ANYWHERE would be throwing them up to the heavens. It's a silly thing to say. It's a problem, isn't it? Sometimes it's hard to be a writer.

"You mean a MILLION years?"

"I didn't say that," Zeus muttered.

"You didn't have to," the bird cawed. "It's as plain as the beak on my face. Prometheus is living in the future. He'll have found those miserable little humans that he loves so much, and he'll be trying to hide among them. But he'll fail."

The monstrous bird spread its wings and flapped. The water in Zeus's foot bowl splashed up his legs, and he cried out. "Careful, you careless cuckoo, you clumsy canary, you stupid starling, you pea-brained pigeon . . ."

The monster wasn't listening. The Fury waddled and skittered over the shiny palace floor, flapped, and at last took off. It shot through the door and vanished into the skies above Olympus.

Hera shook her head. "I hope you're satisfied. You let cousin Prometheus go free, and now you let the Fury hunt him down. You are hopeless, Zeus, hopeless."

The great god's face turned red. He picked up a thunderbolt from the pot beside the throne. "You can't speak to me like that! I am Zeus."

"So what are you going to do about it? The usual?

Lose your temper? Throw thunderbolts around the palace? Zeus, it's time that you grew up," Hera argued.

Zeus hurled a thunderbolt out of the door. Somewhere on Earth a forest was frazzled. "What would YOU do? Huh? You pick faults with ME, but you don't have any better ideas, do you?" he shouted. The shout was enough to cause an avalanche in North America.

Hera folded her arms. "I do."

Zeus scowled. "It won't be a very good idea."

Hera shrugged. "You'll never know, will you?"

"Tell me then," he snapped.

"Say 'please.'"

"No."

"Fine, then you'll spend the rest of time wondering, won't you?"

Zeus threw a thunderbolt, and a small lake in Asia boiled dry. "Oh, get on with it, woman. You know you want to tell me."

Hera sat on the throne next to her husband. "Prometheus loves those humans. He not only gave them fire. He also gave them brickwork, woodwork, the ability to tell the seasons by the stars, numbers, and the alphabet (for writing and remembering things).

He gave them oxen and carriages, saddles, ships, and sails. He gave them healing drugs, gold and silver, and art."

"We could use some art around Olympus," Zeus sighed. "I'd like a nice painting for that marble wall over there. A bunch of sunflowers would be lovely . . . or a woman with a strange smile on her face."

"Zeus?"

"Yes, dear?"

"Shut up and listen."

"Sorry, dear."

"Cousin Prometheus has taken these wonders from heaven and has given them to those humans," Hera said slowly.

Zeus nodded but didn't see where this was leading. "So?"

"So . . . when Prometheus arrives in one million years' time, he will find humans living in the most glorious palaces, sitting by sparkling waters, and eating wonderful food as they listen to beautiful music."

"Music! Yes, we could use some of that in the palace." He threw a thunderbolt, and Earth's tallest mountain became Earth's deepest valley. He listened to the thunderous roar. "Music like that!" he said.

"That was just a clash of rocks, not music," Hera cried.

Zeus pouted. "Crashing rocks is music to me. I like rock music."

"Zeus, will you put down that pot of thunderbolts and listen to what I am saying?"

"Sorry, dear."

"Prometheus is going to arrive in a *heavenly* human world. He stole fire, and he showed you no respect. He needs to be punished."

Zeus spread his mighty hands. "I thought we agreed that chaining him to a mountain and ripping out his liver was a little bit too much?"

"We *did*. He needs a *better* punishment. A punishment to fit the crime. He needs to arrive in a world that is ruined and spoiled. A world where his fire has filled the air with smoke. A place where his little humans have taken their heaven and turned it into a hell."

Zeus nodded. "That's very clever, Hera. I don't suppose that you've thought about how we can arrange that?"

"I have."

Zeus sighed. "I thought you might have." He threw

a playful thunderbolt and wiped out the last herd of woolly mammoths on Earth.

"Zeus! Pay attention."

"Sorry, dear."

ELEVEN

THE STORM INN—JUST A LITTLE BIT LATER

Welcome back. We were in our room at the inn when Uncle Edward mentioned the boy who stood on the burning deck. More about that later. First we had to get to Mucklethrift Manor with our coffin. And a big helper like Theus was going to be very useful.

Theus was so strong that he was able to carry the coffin on his shoulder. Once it was full of Mucklethrift loot, I hoped it would be too heavy for him to carry alone—too heavy meant that we were rich, and Mucklethrift Manor was the best crib that we had ever cracked.[26]

---

26 "Cracking a crib" is the kind of slang used by robbers. The idea is this: we use these funny words so that the police won't understand what we *(cont.)*

He slid the coffin out from under the stage at the end of the Storm Inn barroom. The man with the beard looked over the top of his glasses and sucked on his pipe. It seems that he was a gentleman writer who was touring our country to sell his books.

The gentleman writer had a clever pen that carried its own ink—he called it a fountain pen. It was nice and had a shiny gold nib. Maybe, if we had time, we could steal it from his room before we fled from Eden City. (I am sorry. I can't help myself.)

Ugly little January Storm watched us. She had hate-filled eyes and bottle-filled hands. She was putting the bottles on the shelves, ready for when the customers started to arrive.

She looked like a lizard with a toothache.

We stepped into the damp night air. Fog drifted off the river, and the gas lamps on the street corners did little to chase away the shadows. The shadows were Eden City shadows, and they lapped up light like a hungry cat might lap up a saucer of blood.

26 *(cont.)* are talking about if they are spying on us. "What is cracking a crib?" the spy will ask. "Hey, maybe I have wax in my ears—maybe they are planning to crack a RIB!" And off they will go, thinking that we are harmless when, in fact, we are rotten robbers who are about to break into a building.

We stayed on the wooden sidewalks and stayed out of the way of the carriages that rattled past too fast. If I ever get to be the mayor of a town, I'll make a law against speeding. I'll have traffic policeman on bicycles to catch the culprits and make them pay a fine.

Of course, I'll never be the mayor, so it will never happen.

Gray-faced people hurried through the streets while Theus seemed to wander around in wonder. He looked through the windows of the candlelit rooms. One house looked no bigger than a cottage. Peeling paint was fading on the front wall. It looked as if it had been painted to look like a gingerbread house with cherry cakes and tasty tarts dripping from the sugar-topped roof. I'd seen a cottage like that before. But where?

The paint on the front was faded and dirty. A cracked sign on the door said, "Mrs. Waters's Wonderful World for Children. The Nicest Nursery in Town."

Then I remembered where I'd seen such a cottage before—it was in an old book of fairy tales, and it was a wicked witch's lair.

The windows were thick with grime. With a free hand, Theus rubbed the pane of one window and looked in. I crept under the coffin that he was holding up and peered through.

There were around ten cradles on the bare wooden floor of a dust-thick, spider-webbed room. Each cradle held a pale baby in a grimy shawl. Some were as shriveled as monkeys; some as still as a cod on a block of ice; some making tiny squawks from drooling mouths.

"What's that?" I asked.

Uncle Edward nodded toward the sign on the door. "Mrs. Waters—baby farmer," he read.

"She grows babies? Like a farmer?" Theus whispered. "She can't do that. Only a god can make a human."

Uncle Edward shook his head. "She takes in unwanted babies. She looks after them for the rest of their lives. The parents pay Mrs. Waters to take them off their hands."

"They must pay her a lot—babies need to be taken care of for years."

Uncle Edward has a round and jolly face—strangers meet him, and they want to smile. But that night, in the pale green glow of a gaslight, he looked haunted.

"The babies don't last long in her care," he said. He looked at me. "They soon die. She doesn't have to keep them for long. I found you in the orphanage, Jim. But the orphanage is for children with no parents. The orphanage is bad enough. The baby farms are a hundred times worse."

Suddenly, a door opened into the room full of cribs. The candle flickered, and a woman marched in, like a yellow-haired hag from some fairy tale. She walked over to the crib of a crying baby, shook it roughly, and shouted at the child to go to sleep. Then she looked up suddenly, as if she felt our stares. She turned her red eyes on us and shouted for us to go away.

Theus staggered back and almost dropped the coffin. "Where did I go wrong?" he breathed.

We continued along the sidewalk. "Not your fault, my boy," Uncle Edward said.

"Oh, but it is," Theus said. "I wanted Earth to be heavenly for humans. It was never meant to end like this."

Somewhere in the distant blackness a woman screamed and a cat yowled. The foghorn on the river moaned. "Things look better in the daylight,"

Uncle Edward said.

"They do?" said a voice from down by our feet.

A man lay in a doorway, covered by a thin blanket. His hair was colorless, and his eyes were covered by dark glasses.

"Sorry?" I said.

"Don't say 'sorry'!" the man said, chuckling. "You didn't actually *stand* on me. But if you feel *really* sorry, you could give me some gold—even a piece of silver would buy me a mug of warm beer."

"I don't have any money," I said.

"We don't give money to beggars," Uncle Edward said, tugging on my sleeve.

"Blind beggar, if you don't mind. I'm a poor blind beggar. You can give money to me because I can't see to work."

"I'm sorry," I said.

"That's all right," the blind beggar said. "Watch where you walk. We don't want you dropping that coffin, do we? I may be blind, but I'm still better off than the corpse in that coffin—that's the way I look at it!"

"True," I said. "Good night, sir."

"Good night!" the man cried after us.

We stopped at the street corner. Theus looked at me.

"If he is blind, then how did he know that I was carrying a coffin?"

"He isn't blind," Uncle Edward said.

"He said he was," Theus argued.

"He lied."

"Liars and baby farmers? What kind of world is this?"

We passed the factory gates, where the tops of tall chimneys vanished into the thick night air. The gates of the factory were painted proudly with a name in big golden letters: "Mucklethrift's Machines."

The door swung open, and we saw inside to the ruby-red glow of the furnaces that roared and spewed their smoke. Machines clattered, and wheels whirred and flickered in the red light.

Ragged children staggered out through the gates, coughing and limping. "They've been working fourteen hours with hardly a break," Uncle Edward explained before Theus could ask. He broke into a poem—he knew lots of poems, one for every place we went:

> "Mother, I cannot mind my wheel;
> My fingers ache, my lips are dry:
> Oh, if you felt the pain I feel!
> But, oh, who ever felt as I?"

Then Theus said that curious thing again. "It was never meant to end like this." He added an even stranger thing. "Where are the gods? How could they let this happen?"

What we didn't know THEN was that it was the gods who MADE it happen! And it all began back in Greece one million years ago . . .

TWELVE

GREECE—IN THE PALACE OF ZEUS ON MOUNT
OLYMPUS

*Here we are again. If I'd gone to school, I would have
known this story. Maybe one or two of you readers may
know this story—in which case you can skip to the next
chapter and see what happened at Mucklethrift Manor.
But if you don't know about Pandora, you'd better find out
about Zeus's revenge.*

Hera took Zeus's pot of thunderbolts from him and
held his hand. "Now, husband, we need to sow a little
misery into the human world."

"Yes, dear," he said, growing bored already.

"It will take a woman to do it," Hera said.

"There's a surprise," Zeus muttered. Hera glared at

the great god. He smiled and said, "What is the plan, my sweet?"

"First, we need a woman—a young woman. Get me one."

Zeus reached over to a table beside the throne and picked up a small bell. It clanged.

The clang faded to silence. Nothing happened.

Zeus rang it again. Twice. Clang! Clang!

Zeus sighed. Hera tapped her foot. Nothing happened.

Zeus rang it three times. Four, five, six times— louder and angrier. Something happened.

"All right, all right, all right! I'm coming. Keep your tunic on, Zeus. Good god!"

A young man flew in through the door wearing a small bag at his waist. It hung over his shoulder on a leather strap. He placed a wooden rod by the door— snakes were twined around it. The young man had wings on his sandals and wings on his helmet and a grumpy look on his face. "What do you want this time, you miserable old goat?" the winged man snapped.

Zeus looked annoyed. "I want you to run an errand for me, Hermes, my son."

"Ooooh! Dad wants me to run an errand for him! Anyone would think that I was some kind of messenger boy. Jump here, go there, Hermes! I'll snap my fingers, and you can jump through this flaming hoop, Hermes. Who do you think I am?" he whined.

"You are the messenger of the gods!" Zeus roared and set off an avalanche in the Alps. "It's your *job*, Hermes. You were given *wings* so you could do it. What do you think you are on Olympus for?"

The messenger puffed out his cheeks and thought. "Well, all of the other gods sit around eating ambrosia and drinking nectar, don't they?—when they're not doing godly things," he sniffed. [27]

"Exactly," Zeus said, grabbing the strap on Hermes's bag. "They all *earn* their ambrosia by doing godly things. Poseidon is out there—his job is to look after the sea." He pushed the messenger away from him.

"He makes me sick," Hermes quipped. He laughed

27 Ambrosia, if you don't know or haven't guessed, is the food of the gods. It is the most delicious food you could ever imagine—in fact, the most delicious food you could never imagine. Take all of your favorite foods in one—for me, that would be fried chicken and chocolate ice cream. I once stole some from the kitchen of a rich house, and I've never tasted better since. That would be my ambrosia.

like a braying donkey. "Get it? Sick? Sea? Seasick?"

Hera glared at him, and he smiled back at her. "Cousin Hades is in charge of the underworld," she reminded him. "And that's where you'll be going if you don't obey Zeus."

"Ooooh! The underworld!" Hermes brayed. "People do say that I'm a dead ringer for Hades! Get it? Dead? The land of the dead? Dead ringer?"

"Do I have to remind you about Atlas? His job is to hold up Earth on his shoulders."

"Ooooh! What a backbreaking job," Hermes said, making a face of mock pain.

Hera was furious. "Zeus, hit him with a thunderbolt."

"You took them away from me, my dear," he reminded her quietly.

Hermes looked scared enough and backed away. He tried to keep up the brave act, though. "Ooooh! You gods can't take a joke, can you? Of *course*, I'll deliver your little message, oh great one," he said and fluttered his wings. "What do you want?"

Zeus frowned. "I've forgotten."

Hera leaned forward. "He wants a woman," she said.

"Ooooh! Why would he want another woman when he has someone as beautiful as you, stepmother dearest?" Hermes fluttered.

Hera reached forward and grabbed Hermes by the strap on his shoulder just as Zeus had, but Hera had long fingernails, and they dug into his bare chest. The messenger whimpered. "Listen, stepson. I have had a special woman made. She is in a cave at the bottom of Olympus in a chest marked 'Pandora.'"

"Ooooh! Must be stuffy in there," Hermes said, wiggling and trying to free himself from her grip.

"She is sleeping. Bring her to me," Hera said quietly. "And bring the jar that is in the chest with her. Do you understand?"

"I'm not stupid," Hermes said sulkily.

"If you are not back here in ten beats of a bat's wing, I will get Zeus to throw a thunderbolt into your insolent mouth."

"All right!" Hermes whined. "Let me go! Let me go! I'll be back before you can blink."

Hera blinked.

"Very funny," Hermes said as she released him. He rubbed his pinched skin and flew off down the mountainside.

"Now we need a stupid man," Hera said, looking at Zeus.

"Don't look at me," her husband said.

"Who is the most stupid Titan?" she asked.

"The brother of Prometheus—Epimetheus," Zeus said. "Everybody knows that."

"Exactly—so it is only right that we should get Epimetheus to bring the curse of Prometheus to the humans," Hera said smugly.

The heavenly couple watched as Hermes flew through the door carrying the lifeless form of a beautiful woman and a small jar in his bag. The messenger placed them on the marble floor in front of Zeus, looking warily at the bowl of thunderbolts by Hera's side.

"Can I go now?" he asked.

"No," Hera said sharply. She turned to Zeus. "This is Pandora."

"Beautiful," Zeus said and then caught her glance. "But not as beautiful as you, my dear."

"Beautiful enough for Epimetheus," she said. "I had her made this way. Now, Hermes, my little stepson, breathe into her and give her the gifts of a lying tongue and a cheating heart."

"I don't know what you mean," Hermes huffed.

"Just do it, son," Zeus sighed. The messenger breathed over the resting woman, and a sly look seemed to slip into her sleeping eyes.

It was then Hera's turn to breathe on the young woman. When Hera had done so, Pandora sat up and looked around—slyly.

Hera nodded, pleased with herself. "Girl," she said. "Your name is Pandora, and we have a little job for you."

"Ahh!" The girl smiled like a snake that was about to swallow a mouse. "Goody!"

THIRTEEN

MUCKLETHRIFT MANOR—EVENING

"Aha!" you cry. "The two stories are going their separate ways . . . again." I can see why you may think that. But, in fact, the two stories are about to come together in an unexpected way. So unexpected that I never expected it. No writer could ever think of a twist like this—not even a good writer like me. The fact is that it happens to be true. Back in Eden City we were on our way to Mucklethrift Manor . . .

Theus kept asking "How did this happen?" all the way to Mucklethrift Manor.

"What, Theus?" I asked.

"The liars like that beggar. And the sickness of those babies. The children who are slaves. The gods don't care. Zeus never cared," he muttered and shifted the coffin onto his shoulder and walked on. "Zeus always told me to leave the little hairless humans alone in their cold caves. He said they would soon die out like the dinosaurs. But some of the other gods must have cared. My brother, Epimetheus, cared so much that he went to live with the humans. What went wrong?"

Everything seemed to trouble him—the skinny dogs that fed on gutter scraps, the skinnier girl selling matches on the corner, the smoke from a hot pigeon pie stall, the squabbling men who punched one another into the horse droppings in the middle of the road while gloating groups of grubby women cheered.

The screaming and the steaming of the distant railroad engines made him shiver with horror.

"We need to make a sacrifice," he said as we turned onto Station Street, and I had to skip to keep up with him and Uncle Edward.

"A sacrifice? Kill something?" I gasped.

"Yes. Even in this awful place, there must be a temple. The gods are angry. We have to sacrifice an ox and give the good meat to the gods," he explained. "Where is the temple?"

I shrugged. "Sorry, Theus, Uncle Edward and I only arrived in Eden City a day ago—and we'll be leaving on the midnight train," I said. I could have added "before we get caught." "I don't know my way around the city. But I've never seen a temple in *any* town that we've been to."

He nodded. "That's why the place is so full of evil. But where did it come from?" he asked. He was just about to get the answer.

Uncle Edward reached the front door of Mucklethrift Manor and was about to raise the brass knocker when the wide, shiny door swung open. The butler with the face of an ice pick stood there and waved us in quickly.

The warmth of the house wrapped itself around us. "Aha!" Uncle Edward cried. "We are expected . . . we are welcomed by the master with wine and the finest of your foods, I expect?" he added hopefully.

The butler looked nervous. "Mr. Mucklethrift wants to see you in the library," he said, as worried as a worm on a dry day.

"Of course he does!" Uncle Edward cried. "He wants to talk through my show—maybe share a few stories and a few glasses of fine brandy. I must be a rare treat for a man like Mr. Muckle—"

But the butler cut him off in full flow like turning off a faucet. "Not you, Mr. Slaughter. He wants to see the young gentleman."

"Me?" I squeaked. "What have I done? I haven't done anything! I've never been near his library," I lied, "and I don't have a clue about the silver letter opener that he keeps in the bottom drawer of the desk, and—"

I was cut off even more sharply than Uncle Edward.

"Not *you*, street urchin," the butler sneered. He raised a crooked finger and pointed at Theus. "This young man. I believe your name is Mr. Theus?"

"Yes," Theus answered.

"And Mr. Mucklethrift is your cousin?"

"Well . . ." Theus began. I could see that he was about to say "no."

Uncle Edward cut in. "Indeed, sir, we only employ assistants like Theus if they come from good families. Why, little Jim here is the great-grandnephew of the last king of France."

"Am I?" I blinked.

"Ah, I never told you that," Uncle Edward said.

"I will tell you when you reach your twenty-first birthday."

"Thanks," I said.[28]

"Now, Theus, put the chest in the drawing room so I that can get it ready for tonight's grand show," Uncle Edward ordered, "and then you can run along for a chat with your dear cousin, er . . ."

Theus looked blank.

"George," I added quickly.

"Cousin . . . George?" Theus said.

He carried the coffin carefully into the drawing room and placed it gently on the table. He brushed the dust off his shoulder and the damp off his hat. Then he was ready to follow the butler.

And I was ready to follow him. I am not nosy. I am just curious. Anyway, you should be grateful that I *did* follow them, because I can now tell you what happened next, can't I?

---

28 I have a very good memory. That's why Uncle Edward rescued me from the orphanage. He needed a boy who could learn lots of lines of drama and poetry quickly. I remembered Mr. Mucklethrift's name from earlier in the evening—it was in Chapter Two. I bet you've forgotten that, haven't you? See? That's why I am going to be a great writer and you aren't—probably. Never mind—you can always be a teacher or a garbage collector or do some other awful job.

The butler led Theus along the hallway with the thick, soft carpet and spoke as quietly as his footsteps. "I am sorry. I am confused, Mr. Theus, sir. I was helping Mr. Mucklethrift dress in his room and came downstairs to see to the seats in the drawing room."

"Yes?" Theus said.

"As I passed the library door, Mr. Mucklethrift called me into the library."

"So?"

"So I had left him upstairs just a few moments before. How did he get there?" the baffled butler burbled.

"Don't worry," I said cheerfully. "You are probably losing your marbles."

The butler looked pained. "That's what I thought."

He reached the heavy oak door of the library and tapped before he opened it. The room was dark, except for the light from a single candle. "Come in!" boomed the voice of the man who was Mucklethrift.

Theus stepped in.

While the butler turned to close the door, I slipped around the back of him and into the gloomy room. The door closed, and I was in the shadow of a curtain, where neither Theus nor Mucklethrift could see me.

But the two men were too busy staring at one another to notice a skinny boy like me.

Mucklethrift looked like he did in his portrait. But his body seemed to shimmer—he wasn't so much a rich fat man as a moving picture of one—a ghost, a spirit, a phantom. Or a god trying to take the shape of Mucklethrift.

"Come in, cousin Theus," the shimmering shape said.

"Zeus," Theus sighed. "What are you doing here?" [29]

---

29 See? What did I tell you? You never expected that for one moment, did you? I could NOT make up such a fantastic twist to the plot. That is why it has got to be true. As for the last remark by Theus, that is what you call "a good question." What WAS the top god doing in Mr. Mucklethrift's house . . . and in Mr. Mucklethrift's body? It's another one of those cliff-hangers, I'm afraid. Get on with it.

FOURTEEN

MUCKLETHRIFT MANOR——EVENING, ONE SECOND OR TWO AFTER THE LAST CHAPTER ENDED

You have to remember that I didn't know who Theus and Zeus really were at this stage. I do now. I'll try to report what I saw and heard as if I was just a fly on the wall.[30]

Zeus raised his eyebrows . . . or at least he raised Mr. Mucklethrift's eyebrows. That must have been really hard work because Mr. Mucklethrift's eyebrows were

---

30 Flies on walls don't understand what is going on, of course. And flies have wings—otherwise they'd be called "walks." I don't have wings, or otherwise I'd be called "fly" or "bird" or "pterodactyl" or "bat." So, forget I said that part about the fly on the wall . . . because I've got myself all confused now.

thicker than a thornbush. "Theus, dear cousin, what a way to greet me after one million years," he said and looked hurt.

"You have found me," Theus said heavily. "I suppose that means that the Avenger won't be far behind you."

"Why do you suppose that?"

"Because . . . if YOU found me, then *it* will be able to."

Mr. Mucklethrift's great head shook. "No. I told you. The Fury will only find you if you use godly powers and send a green spark into the sky. I didn't track you down that way."

"How did you find me?" Theus asked.

"The rock and the ring, dear cousin," Zeus said. "As long as you wear the rock and the ring, I can find you wherever you've gone."

Theus looked at the rough gray rock on the dull metal ring and nodded. "What do you want with me?"

Mr. Mucklethrift's shoulders shrugged. "To see how you are doing. To see if there's any chance of you completing your task and finding a human hero."

Theus looked brighter. "I was told that I'll see a

hero at the Storm Inn later tonight," he said. "At least Mr. Slaughter and young Jim are going to tell their tale—then all I have to do is find the boy who stood on the burning deck."

"What if he's dead? These humans don't burn very well, Theus. That's why you should never have given them fire."

"The cave people were *cold*!" Theus argued.

Zeus shrugged Mr. Mucklethrift's shoulders again. "Have you seen what they've done with your fire?" Zeus asked quietly.

Theus hung his head. "The air *is* smoky," he agreed.

Zeus snorted through Mr. Mucklethrift's fat nose. "Smoky? The whole city is wrapped in a blanket of soot and fog. And there are other cities as bad on other continents. One day the smoke–fog–smogs will all join together and smother Earth to death."

Theus looked up angrily. "I may have given the humans fire—but I didn't give them so much misery!" he cried.

Zeus sat back in Mr. Mucklethrift's red leather chair and showed Mr. Mucklethrift's gold-patched teeth in a grin. "No. I did that," the god smirked, pleased with himself.

"Why?" Theus wailed. "Have you seen the suffering on the streets outside?"

"Serves you right, Theus. I let you go free from the rock. But that meant that I had to think of another punishment to teach you and your human pets a lesson."

"What did you do?"

"I had a human woman created named Pandora— a beautiful but selfish and vain girl. Then I sent her to your brother, Epimetheus, with a gift—a beautiful jar."

Theus groaned. "Oh, the fool, the fool! Epimetheus is the most stupid and stubborn Titan on all of Mount Olympus. I told him time and time again. I said, 'Epimetheus, *never*, never take a gift from Zeus. Zeus is the greatest trickster in all of heaven and Earth. Never take a gift from him.'"

Zeus threw back Mr. Mucklethrift's head and showed the forest of hairs up his nostrils. "I know," he snorted, "I know. That's why it was such a joy to do it that way. Pandora went down to Earth—your brother had moved to live with your little human friends, you know."

"I know."

"Pandora was so lovely that he fell in love with her—in spite of her spiteful, greedy nature." Zeus picked up a tobacco jar from the desk and held it in his mighty hand. He mimicked the sweet voice of Pandora. "'Oh, Epimetheus, you are so strong and so handsome. I would love to live with you and be your wife.'"

Zeus then mimicked the voice of Epimetheus—a slow and stupid Titan. Zeus played out the scene between the two.

"'I would love you to be my wife, Pandora, adorable Pandorable.'

'I bring this gift from Zeus as a wedding present.'

'My brother—Prometheus—told me never to take gifts from Zeus. What is it, anyway?'

'It's a jar, sweet Epimetheus. A sealed jar. Zeus said that it is full of riches, but I must never open it. Ever.'

'Right. Put it on the table. It will make a nice decoration.'

'But, Epimetheus, my handsome husband to be, I want to open it.'

'Better not, better not.'"

Zeus explained, "That's when Pandora stamped her pretty feet and wept. She called Epimetheus a cruel and heartless beast. She sobbed that her heart was breaking. She said that if Epimetheus *really* loved her, he would let her open the jar."

"Poor Epimetheus," Theus sighed.

"He could have said 'no,'" Zeus said and then spread Mr. Mucklethrift's fat hands out wide. "But in the end he said 'yes.' And Pandora opened the jar."

"What was inside?" I squeaked.

The god and the Titan seemed to hear me, but they didn't look at where I hid in the shadow of the door.

"When she opened the jar, she let out all the evils of the world. There were sorrow and plague—they leaped from the jar like fleas from a big black rat. They raced through the window and out into the world till it was all infected. Then out jumped bad luck and misery. Pandora screamed, of course, and struggled to put the lid back on the jar. But out pushed lies and despair. They took the world for their own. And THAT is what you saw outside tonight, Prometheus. Your punishment for giving them fire."

My friend shook his head sadly. "Was there nothing good in the jar?"

Zeus leaned forward. "One thing, Prometheus, one thing. The one thing that keeps these little humans going through the hatred and the horrors that surround them. The one thing that those bruised babies grab onto till the end. The one thing that makes the beggar cling to your coattails. The one thing that makes little Jim there think that he will get rich by robbing. And the one thing that makes you think that you'll find your human hero."

Prometheus turned and looked at me as if he was looking at a stranger for the first time. "Do you know what he means?" he asked me. [31]

"There's only one thing that keeps me and Uncle Edward going," I said quietly.

"And what is that?"

"Hope," I said. "Never-ending *hope*."

Zeus clapped Mr. Mucklethrift's hands slowly.

---

[31] Well, dear reader? Do YOU know what keeps us all going in the dark days and darker nights? Do NOT cheat by reading on for the next few lines. This is a riddle. Solve it.

"Well done, boy. The world would have ended in misery a million years ago if it wasn't for *hope*."

Mr. Mucklethrift's body began to shimmer and fade. Soon I could see through it like the grimy-gray window into the baby farm. Mr. Mucklethrift's body began to change shape, too—it was the glorious golden form of a god. He had the ivory wings of a swan. Almost too beautiful to look at—certainly too beautiful to tear away my eyes from.

It was a beauty that made the dreary world of Eden City all the more unbearable. The snicker that usually hid in the shadows was silenced. In the place of the snicker was a shudder. Eden City was afraid.

Zeus smiled a golden smile at me and faded into a golden glimmer.

He was gone. All that was left was the glow of the candle. My head ached as I tried to make sense of what I'd just seen. "Who are you?" I whispered.

After the silence Theus began to talk quickly. He told me the tale of his imprisonment on the Caucasus Mountains, of his escape and his flight to Eden City.

"So you see, Jim, I need to find a hero. If I win my bet with Zeus, then some of Pandora's misery may be lifted from Earth. Can we do it?" he asked.

I nodded. "We can hope," I said.

There was a soft tap at the door, and it swung open.

FIFTEEN

MUCKLETHRIFT MANOR—THE DRAWING ROOM

Go on. Guess who was at the door. Want a clue? All right. It was either the real Mr. Mucklethrift or his butler; it was either Sergeant Sergeant or January Storm. But which one?

The door creaked open, and a face peered around. It was a fat face with hair like the top of a dandelion. When he saw that Theus and I were alone, he stepped into the room carrying a small box that had been in the coffin. "Has Mr. Mucklethrift gone?" he asked.

"Yes, Uncle Edward," I said. [32]

---

32   Well? Did you guess right? What? You thought my clue was misleading? All I can say is that you are a very bad loser. Heh! Heh!

"The guests are gathering," he said. "I have set up the magic lantern and the screen."

"You use magic?" Theus asked.

"Not really, my boy. It is called a magic lantern, but it is just a simple oil lamp. It shines through a picture, and the picture appears on the wall behind us," Uncle Edward explained. "It sets the scene and thrills our audience."

Theus nodded. "I see."

"Did you have an interesting chat with your cousin?" Uncle Edward asked.

"Yes," Theus said with a sigh. "He told me why there is so much misery in the world."

"Huh?" Uncle Edward blinked.

I didn't want Uncle Edward to know the story about Theus. He would only trick the Titan into using his godly powers to make us rich. "You need to put your makeup on, Uncle Edward," I said quickly.

"Ah, true, so true, young Jim." He turned to Theus. "Your cousin won't mind if we use his library as our dressing room, will he?"

"Um . . . no," Theus said with a shrug.

Uncle Edward sat in the chair and wrapped a handkerchief around his neck. Then he opened his makeup box and began to cover his face with greasepaint and powder. As he did so, he explained to Theus, "I need to make myself look like a horrible fat old man."

"But you are a horrible fat old man," Theus said.

"Ha! Ha! Very funny, my boy. When Jim and I do a comedy show, we will use your talent for jokes," he promised. He looked in the small mirror on the inside of the box and gave a great shudder. "Ooooh! Sometimes I even scare myself." He turned to us. "Now, Jim, you know what to do?"

"Yes, Uncle Edward," I said wearily. "I act in the drama of 'The Uncle' . . ."

"That's right. Then, when it's finished, Theus here will carry the coffin out of the drawing room, and Jim will stay in the hall with the coffin."

"Why?" Theus asked. "Why can't I do that?"

"Ah, oh, um . . . Jim likes to 'look after' the coffin. Don't you, Jim?" He gave me a fat wink that said, "When I say *look after*, I mean fill with loot."

"Yes, Uncle," I said. "It's my job."

"Meanwhile, I will recite the poem about the burial of Sir John Moore after Corunna . . ." And Uncle Edward warmed up his voice by practicing the pitiful poem . . .

> *"Slowly and sadly we laid him down*
> *From the field of his fame fresh and gory;*
> *We carved not a line, and we raised not a stone,*
> *But we left him alone with his glory."*

"Fresh and gory?" Theus shuddered. "Don't you know any happy poems?"

"No, no, no, my boy! The customers like a little bit of horror, a little terror, a little suffering."

Theus shook his handsome head. "They seem to have plenty of that in Eden City," he said.

"Ah, but you have only seen the poor suffering masses in the streets and the gutters, young man. Tonight you will see how the rich folks live. Tonight you will see the happy people of this city—and the happy people like a little miserable poetry to remind them how happy they are. See?"

"No," Theus said. He was about to argue when there was a knock at the door again, and it opened.

The butler stood there with winter in his face. "I have two gentlemen to see you," he said and threw the door open even wider.

I froze colder than the butler's nose. I knew who the two men were from their pictures on the walls of the hall. The large man was George Mucklethrift, owner of Mucklethrift Manor. The weedy one was Mayor Walter Tweed.

We were finished. We would be discovered. At least we didn't have a coffin full of Mucklethrift loot yet. Maybe they would throw us out for lying—maybe they wouldn't hang us. But my throat felt tight at the thought anyway.

Mr. Mucklethrift stepped into the room. "Good evening, gentlemen. Welcome to Mucklethrift Manor. I am pleased to have you here. We have one or two ladies who sing to the piano, but . . ." He leaned forward and prodded Uncle Edward in the vest. He lowered his voice, "They sound more like strangled cats, know what I mean?"

The word "strangled" gave me that ache in the throat again.

When Mr. Mucklethrift laughed, he threw back his head and showed the forest of hairs up his nose, just as he had when Zeus had copied his body.

Uncle Edward laughed happily. "Of course, my friend. We will offer your guests something very different. Drama and thrills. A night that they will never forget."

And a night that Mr. Mucklethrift would never forget when he found his house robbed of its valuables.

Mucklethrift laughed with Uncle Edward and said, "Will you be ready to start in ten minutes?"

"Our pleasure and our honor," Uncle replied with a small bow.

"And it must be a special thrill for you to meet your old school friend," Mucklethrift added.

"Must it?"

"Why, yes. He gave you a note yesterday," Mucklethrift said. "My butler told me."

"He did?"

"Of course he did! That's why you're here."

"It is?"

"It is. I wouldn't let just any old stranger into my house." Mr. Mucklethrift turned and wrapped an arm around the shoulder of the weedy man. "Here he is, Mayor Tweed, your old friend. Edward Slaughter. You *said* you wanted to see him."

The weedy mayor looked at Uncle Edward with eyes like a rattlesnake's. "I want to see *Mister* Edward

Slaughter. I most certainly *do*. We have one or two *very* interesting things to say to each other."

I closed my eyes and felt faint.

Mr. Mucklethrift chuckled. "I'll leave you two old chums together," he said. "Don't keep him too long. The show starts in five minutes."

"What I have to say won't take long at all," the mayor said with menace.

Mr. Mucklethrift closed the door and closed us in. This was one pot of hot water that Uncle Edward would not be talking us out of. Still, he smiled bravely. "Come in, my old friend. Come in, Willy."

"It's Wally," I groaned. "His name is Wally."

"Oh, well," Uncle Edward said with a smile.

"Oh, swell," I sighed.

SIXTEEN

THE LIBRARY AT MUCKLETHRIFT MANOR—
A FEW SECONDS LATER

"Get out of that!" you cry. Uncle Edward could talk his way out of chains on the Caucasus Mountains. But this was one very nasty little position to be in. He had talked his way past the butler. But Mayor Walter Tweed was no fool, and he wasn't going to be fooled. We were all heading for the scaffold—but not just yet . . .

"What's your game?" the little mayor demanded.

"Game, my old friend? No game," Uncle Edward laughed. He had a light and happy laugh. It was the laugh he used when he was desperate. "I gave your name to Mr. Mucklethrift so we could perform in his home. We are here to do a show, and then we'll be on our way—no harm done."

"You showed the butler a letter from me," the mayor accused.

"A little forgery. No harm done. I would have come to you for a letter, but you are so important these days . . .".

Mayor Tweed's chest puffed out like a peacock's. "I am," he said.

"And your secretary wouldn't let me in to see you," Uncle Edward lied.

"I'm a very busy man."

"I know. We didn't want to waste your precious time."

"Thank goodness for that."

"We knew that you'd sign the paper if you had time—we just didn't want to trouble you," Uncle Edward finished.

The mayor nodded. "Strictly speaking, you forged my name."

Uncle Edward put on his "ashamed" face and looked at the floor like a naughty child. "I know, Willy."

"Wally," I hissed.

"I know, Woolly."

"Don't let it happen again."

"No, Welly."

The mayor turned the door handle and opened it enough to let the hall light flood in. Uncle Edward raised a fist in victory. The mayor stopped. He turned. He frowned. He squinted his rattlesnake squint. "Hang on," he said.

I wished he hadn't used the word "hang."

"Hang on . . . WHY would I have signed the paper if I'd had the time?" he demanded.

"To say it was all right for us to enter Mr. Mucklethrift's home," Theus added.

Mayor Tweed shook his weedy head. "I mean WHY would I WANT to sign it?"

"Because you were tortured in school with Mr. Slaughter," Theus explained.

"He means," I added quickly, "because you went to school together."

"But I never went to school with this man."

"Yes, you did, Willy," Uncle Edward said and gave that light laugh again.

"I didn't. You're a lot older than me . . ."

"No, I'm not," Uncle Edward replied and looked set for an argument. That would ruin everything.

"He has a lot of makeup on so that he will look old for the show," I explained. "He's really only forty-two," I said.

"I'm only thirty-nine," Mayor Tweed snapped.

"Thirty-nine I am, my old friend," Uncle said with a smile.

"I don't remember your face," he said.

"It's the makeup—and I am an actor—a master of disguise."

"I certainly do NOT remember your name," the mayor said with a grim grin.

"I changed my name—Slaughter is my stage name."

"What's your real name then?" the mayor shot back.

Uncle Edward's mouth opened and closed like a trout in a fishnet, gasping and grasping for some life. "Don't you remember an Edward in your class?" It was that old trick again—get your victim to tell you the answer. It always worked for Uncle Edward.

Mayor Tweed's eyes were as cloudy as the Storm Inn's beer. I knew then that he was a better actor than Uncle Edward. I knew that there was a trap coming, and I couldn't stop it. "I remember that there was an Edward Casper," he said.

"That's me!" Uncle Edward cried and stepped forward to hug Walter Tweed like a long-lost school friend.

The mayor stepped back. He appeared to grow six inches. "There was no Edward Casper in my class," he said coldly. "You are a phony!"

"No!"

"A fraud."

"No!"

"A fake."

"No!"

"And I know who you are. As the mayor of Eden City, *I* pick the men I want on our police force. Sergeant Sergeant is one of my most trusted men. He told me about two tricksters headed for Eden City. A man and a boy wanted for cunning robberies. I guess that's you two," the mayor said in triumph.

"What about me?" Theus asked.

The mayor turned on him. "Hmmm! Don't know about you. Probably some stooge they picked up in a bar to carry away the loot. But you can hang alongside them."

"Thank you," Theus said cheerfully.

"We haven't robbed anyone in Eden City," I said

desperately.

"Not yet, you haven't," the mayor said. "But you are going to."

There was silence in the room. The sound of the hall clock came ticking through the door, along with the sounds of rich folks gathering in the drawing room next door.

"You are going to rob this house," the mayor said. "Tonight. Just as you planned," he added.

"We are?" Uncle Edward asked.

"You'll hang us," I said.

The mayor smiled the smile of a lizard and licked his lips with his reptilian tongue. "Not if you give me half," he said.

Uncle Edward was quick to understand, but Theus was shocked. "You plan to rob your own friend?" he asked.

"I rob the rich because they can afford it," Mayor Tweed said calmly. "Would you want me to rob the poor?"

"No," Theus said, "but . . ."

"Theus, leave us," Uncle Edward ordered. "See that the ladies and gentlemen are in their seats, and tell them that the show will start in two minutes.

Two minutes are all Mayor Tweed and I need to sort out our little . . . problem."

Theus shook his head and left the room. Uncle Edward spoke briskly. "You will keep Sergeant Sergeant off our trail."

"Of course. I will say that my *old school friend* Edward Slaughter is as honest as the day is long. I will tell him that there are reports that the trickster man and a boy were seen getting on the mail train earlier this evening."

"Good. We will take all the valuables we can find and bring them back to our inn," Uncle Edward said. "You can meet us there and take your share."

The mayor looked pleased with that. "Where are you staying?"

"At the Lost Duck," Uncle Edward said.

"Where's that?"

"It's the last inn on the road south."

"I'll find it," Mayor Tweed said.

Uncle Edward opened the door and hurried him into the hall. "We'll meet there at midnight," he said. "Now we must get on with our show."

The mayor stretched out a weedy hand. "A pleasure doing business with you, Mr. Slaughter."

"Edward, please. Old school friends should call each other by their first names, Willy."

"Wally."

"Woolly."

The mayor slipped into the drawing room, where a woman was squawking a song to a tune from a badly played piano. We stood at the door and waited to make our entrance.

"We'll be on the midnight train out of town while he's looking for the Lost Duck," I said.

Uncle Edward looked smug. "Oh, dear, so we will. What a shame."

I would rather have the mayor on my side than against me. Uncle Edward was taking a risk with our necks. A big risk.

"You are planning to double-cross him?" I asked.

Uncle chuckled. "Single-cross him . . . single-cross. I will only do it once."

How right he was. How wickedly right he was.

SEVENTEEN

THE DRAWING ROOM AT MUCKLETHRIFT MANOR—SEVEN O'CLOCK

I hope that you're as excited now as I was then. Doing a show always made me nervous—would I forget my lines? Then there was the robbery afterward—would I be caught? But now I had Mayor Walter Tweed to worry about—would he betray us? Would he catch us when we tried to single-cross him? And I was still dazed at the thought of meeting a Greek Titan, Theus, and seeing the awesome Zeus. What do you do when your mind is a whirlpool? Swim it one stroke at a time. Get through the show first . . .

The drawing room smelled like cigar smoke and perfume. A fire blazed in the huge hearth, and

Theus looked miserable.[33]

The singing lady stopped her screeching, and the audience clapped. I think they were being kind.

Mayor Walter Tweed jumped onto the low platform where our coffin lay on the table. In back of the coffin was the magic lantern, and I slipped behind the mayor to turn up the wick on the lamp. A picture of a gloomy house was thrown onto the white sheet that we'd hung behind it. The picture would change from time to time as we told the story of "The Uncle."

Mayor Tweed smiled a weaselly smile and spoke some weaselly words to the rich folks gathered in the room. "Oh, Mrs. Popplewhite, thank you so much for your delightful song. I think we can all agree that we have never heard anything like it."

The people in the audience murmured that they had truly heard nothing like it. Maybe if they had worked in a butcher's shop they'd have heard something like her singing—the sound of a pig being killed. But the people in the room didn't look like the type who killed pigs.

---

33   Theus didn't give fire to humans so that they could smoke cigars and pipes. Human beings are clever creatures—that's why Theus loved them. (*cont.*)

"Now," Mayor Weed[34] went on, "It is my huge pleasure, my honor, my privilege, to introduce our next guests. They are Mr. Edward Slaughter and his nephew, little Jim." Suddenly, he tilted his head to one side and asked, "What do we get if we take the 'S' from Slaughter?'"

"Lorter?" Mr. Mucklethrift said from the front row.

Mayor Tweed shook his head, a little annoyed that his joke had been killed. "We get 'laughter,'" he explained. "Laughter and tears from these masters of the dramatic art."

He then launched into a speech that took around ten minutes about how he had gone to school with Uncle Edward and what a young star my uncle had been in those days. It was all lies. But Mayor Tweed was a politician, and lying is what they do best.

At last, he stepped down and left the platform to us.

33   (cont.) But there are some humans who are so stupid that they choose to set fire to tobacco sticks. Maybe clever humans should go around with buckets of water and pour them over these smoke suckers?

34   I really must stop calling him Weed. But I can't help myself. It's like going into a bar where there is a brass spittoon in the corner and a sign: "Please do not spit on the floor." You KNOW you shouldn't do it—but you just can't stop yourself from spitting on the floor, can you? I'll bet you've spat on dozens of floors. So don't blame me for my little wickedness with Weed.

The butler turned down the gas lamps in the room.

Our ancient wooden chest lay on the table, looking black in the shadows. The only light came from the oil lamp in the magic lantern and the flames from the fire. I pushed the slide to change the picture; we now saw a view inside the gloomy house. On the dining room wall was the portrait of a pale but lovely woman.

I looked at her and sniffled, "Mama! My dear, sweet, good mama!"

"Ahh," the audience sighed, and I knew that they would sob and dribble over our sad tale.

Uncle Edward turned to me, his eyes rolling and showing the whites, like some horse with a bad belly. Then his character—a cruel and cold old man—told me the story of my poor parents.

Uncle Edward had loved my mother, he said, but she had married his brother (my father) instead. Then my father disappeared mysteriously, and they never found his body. But Mama knew who had killed him, and she died of a broken heart, as you would too.

Uncle rested his hand on the long black box. He hooked a finger at me. "Come here! You've often tried to open this old chest! It has a secret spring; the touch is known to me alone!" He pressed the button on the end of the box, and I stepped back, waiting for the lid to spring open.

Nothing happened.

Uncle rolled his eyes a little more and cried, "It has a secret spring; the touch is known to me alone," and pressed the button harder.

Nothing happened.

As I leaned closer to the old chest, he placed a hand on the back of my neck and pulled me near so that his mouth was next to my ear and his thick beard tickled my neck. His soft voice hissed in my ear, "I thought I told you to oil that confounded lock, Jim!"

"I did! I did! I did!" I squeaked. "Give it a kick, Uncle Ed!"

He pulled back his thin, gray, greasepaint lips and showed me his gleaming teeth in a snarl, framed by his thick brown beard. He held my head over the chest. "It has a secret spring; the touch is known to me alone!" he roared and kicked the switch. The lid sprang up and smacked me in the nose . . . as he hoped it would.

There was a gasp from one of the ladies in the

room, though I swear that I heard some of the men begin to chuckle.

Slowly, on a spring, a skeleton rose from the coffin and sat up. A woman screamed. There was always one.

While I wiped the blood off my nose, Uncle Edward turned to fix the audience with a glare. They fell silent. "What do you see that makes you groan so heavily?" he asked me and pushed my head toward the open chest.

I sniffled, swallowing blood.

"What do you see that makes you *groan* so heavily?" he repeated.

I groaned.

He pointed to the box. "The thing is just a bare-ribbed skeleton!" he said in a sneering voice.

"Papa!" I wailed, but with a nose full of blood, it sounded more like "Bu-baa."

I staggered away from the hideous skeleton toward the table. There I pushed the slide on the magic lantern, and the picture changed to a gruesome ghost. Uncle Edward fixed his gaze on the glowing shape and gave a terrified cry, "Oh, God! It is my brother, returning from the grave!"

He fell to the floor in a swoon. I stood over the

trembling form and recited my closing lines:

> *"That night they laid him on his bed, in raving*
>   *madness tossed;*
> *He gnashed his teeth, and with wild oaths, he*
>   *cursed the Holy Ghost.*
> *Before the light of morning broke, a sinner's*
>   *soul was lost."*

And with a gurgle in his throat, Uncle Edward died for the first time that night.

There was a hush, and then the butler turned up the gas lamps. The 30 or so ladies and gentlemen burst into cheering and applause. I smiled shyly, but they didn't see me because Uncle Edward jumped up from his deathbed, stood in front of me, and spread his arms out wide. "Thank you, my friends, thank you! You are too kind!"

The audience rose from their fine chairs, embroidered in green and gold, and cried, "Bravo!"

When the applause finally died down, Uncle Edward said, "And that concludes the first part of tonight's show. I beg your patience while my assistant removes the old chest."

He waved at Theus, who stepped forward, picked up the coffin, and carried it out through the door.

"Thank you for being such a wonderful audience, and remember . . . if you see an old locked chest, then don't be surprised if you find a corpse inside it!"

The audience laughed and moved to the side, where servants held trays of champagne and small plates of food. Mr. George Mucklethrift stepped toward Uncle Edward. He was even fatter than Uncle, and his eyes disappeared into slits of fat on his balloon face.

"A triumph, Mr. Slaughter, a triumph! The best night's entertainment I think we've ever had in our parlor!"

"Too kind, too kind," Uncle said. "After the break I will recite 'The Burial of Sir John Moore After Corunna' . . ." he went on.

The fat factory owner frowned. "We don't want to keep my guests from their dinners," he said.

"Ten minutes," Uncle Edward said. He caught my eye as he repeated it. "Ten minutes—not a second more, not a second less."

He pulled out the watch in his vest pocket. "It is seven-twenty now—your guests will go to dinner at seven-thirty."

I understood. The ticking of the clock in the hall would tell me when my time was up. I slipped out to rob the house.

I didn't know then that this would be our last robbery. Ever.

EIGHTEEN

ANCIENT GREECE AND EDEN CITY

I just want to take you back to Theus's home for a moment. I don't want you to think that things had been standing still back in ancient Greece while we were doing the robbery. Things were happening that were going to change our lives one million years later.

The Fury landed with a clatter of claws on the marble floor of the palace and stalked across the room. One of the palace pets sat there chewing on three bones— one for each head. This was the Chimera—one of the creatures that the gods used for rampaging around the world and horrifying humans . . . just for fun.

The Chimera had three heads—lion, goat, and snake. [35] Its body was also mixed, having the front part of a lion, the middle of a goat, and the tail of a snake. It wasn't pretty, and it wasn't the sort of monster that you'd want to meet in an alley at night. To be honest, you wouldn't want to meet it in the daytime either.

It had just returned from a country called Lycia, where it had been killing cattle and terrifying tots. "What do you want?" the lion head asked the Fury.

"I want Zeus," the big bird said.

"He wants Zeus!" the snake head said to the goat.

"He wants some soup?" the goat head bleated.

"Zeus!" the snake head hissed.

"Bless you," the goat head said.

"I am looking for our leader," the Fury said.

"What for?" the lion head asked.

"None of your business," the Fury snapped.

---

35 Being born with three heads is no fun, so do not mock the Chimera. When one of those heads is a goat head, then it is a real nightmare. I mean, have you ever smelled a goat's breath? Imagine being stuck next to that for all of your life. No wonder the Chimera was bad tempered. By the way . . . do NOT try smelling a goat's breath to check what I say. If you die as a result, you will NOT be given your money back for this book.

"In that case, we won't tell you, will we?" the snake snapped back.

"We won't," the lion and the goat agreed.

The Fury closed its eyes and tried to hold its temper. Finally, it opened them and said calmly, "If you will help me, then I'll find a whole city for you to attack and terrify," it promised. "I am tired. I have been circling Earth for a thousand years, and I haven't tasted liver in all that time. Help me, and I'll give you that city."

"Excuse me," the goat head gurgled. "Who's calling me silly?"

"Goat head," the lion groaned. "You are deaf."

"Death?"

"Deaf!" the lion head roared.

"I know. It's all your roaring. Wrecked my ears," the goat head replied.

"Shut up, and let's hear what the Fury has to say," the snake head pleaded.

"It wasn't me that interrupted. It was the goat!" the lion head argued.

"A coat? Yes, I could use a coat. There's a draft in here," the goat head said.

"Have you seen Zeus?" asked the Fury.

"Shoes? Horses wear shoes. But we're the Chimera. You can't put shoes on our goat's feet, can you, Lion?"

"Shut up!" the lion head roared.

The goat head blinked. "Sorry, I'm sure. I was only trying to help," it muttered.

The lion head went on, "Anyway, Zeus isn't here. He went off into the future to see his cousin."

The Fury hopped forward. "How far into the future?" it demanded.

The lion head yawned and said, "I happened to hear Hermes talking to Hera. Zeus was having some new wings made by his son Hephaestus."

"That ugly young god," the Fury said and nodded.

"Yes," the snake head hissed. "Twisted and broken legs from when Zeus once flung him off the mountain. In fact," the snake head added slyly, "his legs are as twisted as your neck. How did that happen, Fury?"

"That's not important," the big bird snarled. "What did Zeus say to Hephaestus?"

"Oh, he said that he wanted the wings to be strong enough to take him one million years into the future," the lion head replied.

"Yes, I heard him say that," the snake head said.

"I didn't hear him say that," the goat head added sadly.

The Fury was confused. "You DIDN'T hear it? Are you saying that he's lying?"

"Of course, he's a lion. And the other one's a snake," the goat head said.

The monster bird shook its feathers. "Thank you, Chimera. ONE million years, eh? I haven't been looking *that* far into the future." He shuffled to the window ledge and got ready to take off. "Thanks. It's been great."

"A grape?" the goat head bleated.

"Shut up," the lion and the snake bellowed as the Fury took off again.

★★★

Meanwhile, in Mucklethrift Manor, I was speeding through the rooms. I had a large felt sack— the thick material muffled the clank of the silver and gold as I dropped things inside. I took time to close all the drawers and cupboards after I'd emptied them. With luck, no one in the manor would notice the missing loot till we were far away in another city.

Servants were busy in the long dining room, setting the table for the guests. Just one of those silver teaspoons would have kept the match girl in bread for a month. But I knew everyone would be heading straight for the dining room. If I took anything, then it would be missed very quickly and spoil the getaway plans.

I went into the library, where the aura of Zeus still hung in the air somehow—like a dream after you've woken up. I dropped all the most precious things inside the bag and sped back into the hallway. One minute had ticked by. I took each of the other rooms at the same steady pace—I didn't race and make mistakes, but I didn't drag my feet.

There was a room where guests had hung their coats. I took one more precious minute to go through wallets and purses to slip out a little cash—so much cash from such rich people. I didn't empty any of the wallets completely, or the owners would have missed their money and called the police—just a few bills and coins from each one.

When I'd finished downstairs, five minutes had gone on the clock. As the hand crept to seven twenty-five, I raced to the coffin and pressed the button to open the lid. It didn't move. I'd oiled it, I swear I had. I gave it a kick, and at last it swung open.

The skeleton sat up, and I pushed him farther forward. There was a deep space underneath him, and I slipped the heavy bag inside, out of sight. I pushed the cash into a pocket under Skinny the skeleton's head. I pulled a second bag from the coffin and ran to the stairs. I went up two at a time. I had four minutes—no more, no less.

The bedrooms and bathrooms were empty now that the servants were all worrying about dinner for 30 guests. I must have missed a fortune inside the handbags and jewelry boxes on the dressing tables, but some ruby rings, an emerald bracelet, and diamond cuff links were real treasures.

I tore out onto the landing and heard a creak at the bottom of the stairs. The great clock was winding itself up to chime the half hour. I threw myself onto the banister and slid down it. I landed almost on top of the coffin.

Ding-dong, ding-dong, went the clock.

I kicked the button, and the skeleton rose.

Ding-dong, ding-dong! The clock finished chiming. The door of the drawing room opened slowly.

Uncle Edward peered around and saw me struggling to stuff the second sack in and slam down the lid on the bony skull. His face was red.[36] Even under the greasepaint and powder, I could see that he was hot and worried.

He pulled Theus out after him and whispered, "Get that chest out of here and back to the Storm Inn *now*."

Theus obeyed and put the heavy box on one shoulder.

Mr. Mucklethrift threw the door open wider to let his guests out to the dining room, and the rich folks pushed past me and flattened me against the wall in their greed to get to their feed.

"Sorry about that," Mr. Mucklethrift said, throwing an arm around Uncle Edward's shoulder. "Are you sure that you wouldn't like to join us for dinner?"

Uncle Edward had the magic lantern wrapped in the cloth that we used for a screen, and he tucked it under his arm.

---

36 Uncle Edward's face was red—not the skeleton's. The skeleton was as white as ivory. Uncle Edward said that it was a skeleton stolen from a hospital. The doctors had used it to teach students about how the body works. Of course, the skeleton had been a living man once. It had probably come from a criminal who had been hanged. Poor man. I hoped that I wouldn't suffer the same fate. Some hope.

"No, Mr. Mucklethrift," he said. "Another show to do before the night is out."

Mr. Mucklethrift shook hands with Uncle Edward. "Good night then, Slaughter. A pleasure to have met you. I hope that you'll come again some evening?"

"Of course. I look forward to seeing you again soon," Uncle Edward lied.

Of course, we didn't plan to see Mr. Mucklethrift *ever* again. Little did we know that we would—and not in his drawing room.

NINETEEN

THE STREETS OF EDEN CITY

I can't begin to describe Eden City at night. The people, the sounds, the smells—especially the smells. Well, I COULD begin to describe it, but it would make you sick. Just take my word for it—Eden City was not the sort of place where you would want to go for a picnic. But we didn't plan to live there. And I certainly didn't know that I would almost die there . . .

The air of Eden City was thicker than ever as we hurried through its stinking streets. It was trying to hide something from us. It wanted to confuse us and lose us. I was suddenly afraid that the city would stop us from reaching the safety of the station and the midnight train.

But it didn't stop us from reaching the Storm Inn.

A few people looked at Theus curiously and wondered why he was carrying a coffin, but no one tried to stop us. No one ran behind us, shouting, "Stop, thieves!"

"Uncle Edward," I asked, "why did Mr. Mucklethrift say 'sorry' as you left the room?"

"Ahhh!" Uncle Edward sighed as he strode out and left me skipping to keep up with him. "We had a little problem in the drawing room while you were . . . er, *exploring* Mucklethrift Manor."

"Your uncle had to work very hard to keep the guests in there for ten minutes," Theus said.

"You mean I was almost caught? What went wrong? 'The Burial of Sir John Moore After Corunna' always takes ten minutes," I argued.

"Sadly, they would not let me recite that poem. It seems that the granddaughter of Sir John was one of the guests. We had already upset her when Skinny the skeleton popped out of the coffin. She said that she would faint if we told the story of her dear old grandfather."

"So, what *did* you do?" I demanded.

"I did 'The Daffodils,'" he said.

"But that doesn't last ten minutes," I argued.

"I know. That left me with two minutes to fill. Two minutes to save my neck from the hangman's rope," he moaned.

"What about my neck?" I asked.

Uncle Edward looked annoyed. "If they hang me, you'll be left alone in this world. You will starve. You will die slowly and in misery. It is important that MY neck is saved. Otherwise they may as well hang you."

"Thanks, Uncle," I muttered.

"Anyway, someone asked me to do the poem about the sinking of *The Revenge*," he went on.

"That takes twenty minutes," I said.

"Exactly. You would have been sitting by the coffin for ten whole minutes. Ten minutes in which the theft could have been discovered. I had to get out and save our necks."

"So what did you do?"

"I told them I couldn't do a poem about the sea. I said I was terrified of drowning—even in Mucklethrift Manor, I was terrified of drowning. A man called out, 'But we are two miles from the sea!' I replied, 'Exactly, sir . . . that makes it all the more difficult for the lifeboats to get to me!'"

"They must have thought that you were crazy," I laughed.

"Perhaps they did—but at least it passed the two minutes you needed, my boy. Did we make a fortune?" he asked.

I was just about to list the things that I'd stolen when I noticed that there was something missing. We had stopped at a crossroad. A boy even smaller than me stood there with a broom made out of twigs. He was sweeping the horse droppings into the gutter so that people with nice shoes could cross without getting them dirty. I looked around. Something was definitely missing. Then I knew what it was.

Theus. Where was Theus?

"Uncle!" I cried. "Where's the coffin?"

He stopped and looked around wildly. "The thief! The villain! The rogue! He has run off with our treasures. I knew he was not to be trusted. Never trust a man with long hair," he moaned. He tucked the magic lantern under his left arm and grabbed me by the lapel of my coat with his free hand. "You were supposed to be watching him, Jim."

"Me?" I squeaked.

"You let me down," he said and slowly lifted me up till his nose was a hand's width away from mine. "Unless you were in this plot together. A plot to rob this poor old man of his worldly treasures."

I was angry. Angry at being tricked by Theus. Angry at being suspected by Uncle Edward. "Now look here!" I yelled in his face and squirmed. "You are NOT a poor old man—you are a middle-aged thief. You did NOT tell me to watch him. And he has NOT robbed you of your worldly treasures—he has robbed us of Mr. Mucklethrift's worldly treasures."

"Same thing, my boy," he said and let me drop on the wooden boardwalk with a clatter.

The little crossing sweeper looked up at us with interest. "Are you thieves then? Have you just robbed Mucklethrift Manor?"

"Big mouth," I moaned at Uncle Edward.

"Ah, no, little crossing sweeper. We are undertakers, aren't we, Jim?" he said, turning to me.

"Are we?"

"We are. And we have just come from Mucklethrift Manor, where an old servant has died. We were taking the body away to the chapel of rest, weren't we, Jim?"

"Were we?" I sniffed. I was still annoyed.

"We were. And the careless pallbearer seems to have gotten lost," Uncle Edward said.

"You are thieves," the crossing sweeper said. "Pay me, or I'll tell Sergeant Sergeant all about you. He's due here any minute. He's like clockwork."

Uncle Edward drew in a deep breath. "I will not be blackmailed. Especially not by someone so short that he has to stand on a ladder to tie his shoelaces," he boomed at the boy.

"I don't have shoelaces. I don't have shoes," the boy replied. "Ma just blacks my feet and laces up my toes!"

"You will not get a penny from me with threats," Uncle Edward said grandly.

"Fine. Then will you pay me if I tell you where your friend with the coffin went?" the skinny boy asked and wiped his grubby hand across his nose.

"You know?"

"'Course," the boy said with a nod.

Uncle Edward searched in his pocket and pulled out a small piece of silver. He passed it over. The boy bit the coin to make sure that it wasn't a cheap forgery made out of tin and then slipped it into the pocket of his ragged pants. He pointed back the way that we had just come. "He turned into the last alley."

Uncle Edward spun around and stomped back down the boardwalk. I hurried after him. Then Uncle stopped suddenly.

The alley was a cobbled path that ran between two tall wooden buildings. A sign at the end said: "To the Temple of the Hero."

The coffin was propped up against a wall near where the alley met the main street. The light from the street corner didn't shine very far into the alley. It was as gloomy as a whale's belly. I could see Theus standing there. I could also see why he had stopped. He was talking to Sergeant Sergeant.

I gasped. "He's not a thief trying to steal our loot," I whispered.

"No," Uncle Edward murmured. "He's worse. He's a police spy."

"We're done for, Uncle. Done for."

TWENTY

THE STREETS OF EDEN CITY

I am feeling kind. I will NOT take you back to ancient Greece in this chapter. You want to know what happened when Theus met Sergeant Sergeant, don't you? Of course you do. I mean to say, I could tell you the important thing that was happening back on Mount Olympus, but you don't want to hear that now, do you? You do? Look, reader, you can't have it both ways. Let's sort out Theus first.

"He told me that he was a Titan," I moaned.

"What?" Uncle Edward blinked.

"Nothing, Uncle." I felt so ashamed that I had been taken in by that Olympus nonsense. Of course a Titan and a god wouldn't show up in Eden City.

"I will use my usual skills to talk us out of trouble,"

Uncle Edward said.

"Yeah. Like you talked us out of trouble with Mayor Tweed," I reminded him. I still felt sore from where he'd grabbed my jacket and lifted me up off the ground.

"Police spy, is he? We'll see about that!" Uncle placed the magic lantern on the end of the standing coffin, put on his bravest smile, and marched across to Sergeant Sergeant.

"Ah, Sergeant, I see you have met my young friend."

Then I remembered.

"Yes," the policeman replied. "He was just asking me."

I remembered Zeus.

"Do not believe a word this young man says!" Uncle continued.

"Uncle!" I cried.

"Young Theus had a knock on the head when he fell on the floor at the inn, didn't you, Theus?"

"He's not a police spy!" I cried.

"Yes," Theus said. "I did fall over at the Storm Inn."

"And the blow to the head has had a strange effect on him. He has nightmares," Uncle Edward was saying. "And in these nightmares he imagines that he's a member of a gang of thieves . . ."

"No, he doesn't, Uncle!"

"What?"

"Theus is our friend," I said.

"A friend who has had a knock on the head and is now our enemy," Uncle argued hotly. "He will tell you lies, Sergeant, in order to see us hang!"

The policeman shook his head wearily, and the mist that had gathered on his drooping mustache dripped onto the cobbles. "He was just asking me about the temple," he said.

"We are simple entertainers, and we have not just robbed Mucklethrift Manor," Uncle said and then stopped. He suddenly seemed to hear what the policeman had said. "Temple? What temple?"

"The Temple of the Hero," the policeman said. "It's a small temple at the end of the alley. Some weird people worship some sort of god there. Something about him dying to save his friends. A hero, they call him. They worship him in the hope that he'll come back."

Theus nodded. "I *need* to find a hero," Theus said. "It will change the world if only I can find one good man."

"Like I told you, son," the policeman said, "the hero is dead. There's no use going to the temple—it's closed tonight anyway. No use coming back in the morning either."

"I can't come back in the morning anyway. I'm taking the midnight train," Theus said.

"No," Sergeant Sergeant said, "I mean it's no use coming back ANY time. This hero died a few hundred years ago."

Theus nodded. "Then I'll just have to go back and find him before he dies."

The policeman looked at Uncle Edward. He spoke softly. "I see what you mean about the knock on the head. Better get him back to your lodgings. Do you have you far to go?"

"The Storm Inn," Theus said.

"NO!" Uncle all but shouted. "The Lost Duck . . . we're staying at the Lost Duck! See, the knock on the head really scrambled his brain."

Sergeant Sergeant shook his head sadly. "Take care of him," he said.

Uncle Edward took one arm, and I took the other. My knees were weak with fear. I wasn't so much leading Theus out of danger as I was hanging onto him to stop myself from falling in a heap of quivering terror.

Uncle Edward picked up the magic lantern, and Theus put the coffin on his shoulder again. We reached the end of the alley.

"Hey!" Sergeant Sergeant called.

We stopped. We turned.

"I've never heard of the Lost Duck, and I've lived in Eden City all of my life," the policeman said.

"Just built it," I said quickly.

"Where?"

"Last inn on the road south."

"Ah."

We stepped into the gloomy green glow of the gaslit main street.

"Hey!" Sergeant Sergeant called again.

We stopped. My knees wobbled again.

"Yes, Sergeant?"

"You're heading north."

"Ah, yes," Uncle Edward explained. "We have another show to do before we go back to the Last Duck."

"The LOST Duck," Sergeant Sergeant said.

"Where?"

"Where what?"

"Where is this duck that's lost?" Uncle Edward asked.

"It's the last inn on the road south," the policeman said.

"So, it's the LAST duck, isn't it?" Uncle Edward said with a chuckle.

Sergeant Sergeant tugged at his mustache. "I guess it is." He saluted us. "You folks take care now," he said. "There are one or two ruffians on the streets who'll rob you of everything you have," he warned us.

Uncle Edward turned and faced him. "While you are walking these mean streets, Sergeant, I feel very safe. Good night."

"Good night, sir," he replied.

At last we were free, and we hurried down the road. The little crossing sweeper called cheerfully, "You got away with it then?"

Uncle Edward stepped on the boy's bare toes to teach him a lesson.

We passed the Mucklethrift factory and the match girl who was huddled in the gateway. She'd wrapped the shawl around her shoulders and fallen asleep. Uncle Edward reached into the coffin, took out a handful of coins, and slipped them into her wallet. He could be the meanest man in the world. He could also be the kindest. Like Robin Hood, he would rob the rich and give to the poor. He didn't deserve to die on the end of a rope.

As the distant town hall clock boomed eight o'clock, we reached the waterfront, where the Storm Inn sat like a wooden toad on the edge of the slimy river.

TWENTY-ONE

OLYMPUS (AT THE DAWN OF TIME) AND THE STORM INN

You probably think that it's easy for me to fly backward and forward through time with my story. It's not. It's a little bit like putting Skinny the skeleton together—I have all the pieces, but I have to put them in the right order. Now I just need to keep things in order by going back to ancient Greece for a few minutes.

Zeus raged and Zeus roared. Zeus reached into his pot for a thunderbolt to throw, but the pot was empty. That made Zeus angrier.

"Hermes!" he cried.

The messenger with wings on his helmet and wings on his sandals fluttered forward. "No need to shout. What do you want now?"

"I want you to get Pegasus, my winged horse," Zeus fumed.

"Ooooh! Those stables are so smelly," Hermes said and turned up his fine nose. "Couldn't you send the Chimera?"

Zeus's eyes looked like thunderbolts as he gazed at his flying son. "I want the Chimera *here*, where I can keep its flapping mouths shut. And I want you to do as you are told, just for once. Bring me Pegasus."

"But, Father," Hermes said with a sigh, "I am a faster flier than that old feathered nag. Why not send *me*? I need a vacation. A nice little trip away from Olympus. Somewhere warm with sandy beaches and waving palm trees—" [37]

Zeus cut in. "I want someone to go down to the underworld and bring me a pot of thunderbolts."

Hermes stopped his flapping. "The underworld? Hades? Ugh! All those screaming and tortured souls?

[37] That's something you NEVER see in myths and legends—gods going on vacation. I mean, they must have done it, but no one ever writes about it. Even Uncle Edward and I used to go fishing for a couple of weeks every summer. It makes you wonder, doesn't it? No? All right, it makes ME wonder.

No, thank YOU! And, anyway, I carry messages—not big dirty pots of heavy thunderbolts. I'll strain my sandal wings. Ooooh, no! Tell you what . . . I'll go and get Pegasus for you." And he sped through the door with a buzz like a hummingbird.

Hera turned to Zeus with a frown. "I wonder if those human creatures have this sort of problem with their children?"

Zeus shook his head. "They send babies to baby farms if they don't like them. And, when they grow up, they collect the children all together in pens. They call them 'schools.'"

The queen of the gods looked shocked. "How sad. I suppose it was my fault for sending Pandora with her jar of troubles?"

Zeus shook his head. "I don't remember a trouble called 'school' in Pandora's jar—maybe it was mixed up with the general misery."

Hera looked a little guilty. "Are you sure you want to help these human beasts?"

Zeus spread his hands. "They are funny little things. I can see why cousin Prometheus likes them and wants to help them." He turned his gaze on the Chimera. "That is why I am so angry with the

Chimera. The three heads without a brain between them. They only went and betrayed Theus to the Fury, didn't they?"

The snake head writhed. "It was an accident. It just sort of slipped out . . . out of the lion's mouth."

The lion turned its head and roared at the snake head. "That's right, blame me!"

"Well, *you* told the Fury that Prometheus was headed one million years into the future, didn't you?" the snake snapped back. "If Zeus is going to hit a head with a thunderbolt, then it's your head that gets it, pal."

"I'll blow off ALL of your heads if you don't stop squabbling," Zeus roared, louder than the lion head.

"You'll show us all to our beds?" the goat said with a grin. "Thank you. I could use a nap."

Zeus groaned and jumped to his feet as Pegasus folded its wings and shot through the open window. Its smooth hooves skidded across the marble floor, and it headed straight for Hera's throne. Luckily for her, it smashed into the Chimera first, and a tangle of heads and wings, fur and feathers, rolled over the palace floor.

Zeus grabbed a hoof and pulled Pegasus free.

"Oh," the lion head groaned. "That creature is a menace on the ground."

"It should have a warning to let everyone know that it's coming," the snake head agreed.

"Yes, Zeus, give it a horn!" the lion head roared.

"It can have one of mine," the groggy goat head groaned. "I've got a pair of horns."

The lion head and the snake head turned toward the goat head. "Shut up!" they bellowed.

Zeus threw himself onto the back of Pegasus. "I'm tired of all this flying," he said. "Pegasus can take me to Eden City this time."

"What about the thunderbolts?" Hera asked.

"No time for that. I've got a feeling that Theus may need me soon," Zeus explained and guided Pegasus to the windowsill. "Come on, Peg!" he cried as they leaped out over the mountainside. "Time to head off."

The goat head blinked. "Head off? Which head is coming off?"

The lion looked at the snake, and the snake looked at the lion.

"Oh, I hope it's yours," the lion sighed. "I *so* hope it's *yours*."

Meanwhile, at the Storm Inn, we pushed through the swinging doors into the crowded and smoke-filled room. It was full of noise—men and women laughing and arguing, eating and drinking, cursing and taunting. The room smelled like an unwashed armpit . . . but that could have been January Storm's stew, which was bubbling in bowls and smelled like dead cats rotting. She was trotting from table to table serving, so she had no time to make any spiteful remarks as we walked in.

Her father was serving behind the bar, slopping clouded brown beer into dull pewter mugs.[38] The gentleman writer was still sitting at the window table writing away with his fountain pen. He waved at us as we pushed through the crowd to the side of the stage to stow away the coffin and the loot.

Theus checked that his swan wings were still safe while Uncle Edward went up to our room to make sure that our bags were packed. We wanted a fast

---

38 January would never tell me what happened to her mother. She didn't live at the Storm Inn, but even January must have had a mother. I think that January was ashamed of what had happened to her. Maybe her mother was in prison/hiding/heaven.

getaway in time to catch the midnight train.

I changed into my sailor's uniform while Uncle Edward set up some new slides in the magic lantern— slides of a stormy sea and a burning ship.

One or two bleary-eyed, beery-eyed customers watched us and leered. I could tell that they were planning to give us a hard time. But we'd played to worse crowds—once we had to play to 1,000 children in a small-town theater. They were wilder than a jungle full of monkeys.

Mr. Storm barged his way through the crowd and said, "Time for you to put on a show."

"Thank you, my good man," Uncle Edward said. "Would you care to introduce us to the ladies and gentlemen?"

Mr. Storm glared at him. "There are no ladies or gentlemen in this room—except maybe that writer feller." But he turned to the crowd and shouted, "Get yourselves seated, and listen to tonight's act."

The mob of grubby faces turned toward us. Mr. Storm went on, "They aren't very good, but they're the best we can afford. I present to you Mr. Edward Slaughter and little Jim, who are going to perform . . . what are you going to perform?"

"'The Boy Stood on the Burning Deck,'" Uncle Edward reminded him.

"'The Boy Stood on the Burning Deck!'" Mr. Storm called, and there was some feeble clapping.

Suddenly, a man with a beard and a glass eye jumped to his feet and cried, "Hey! I know that one!" As the customers cheered, he jumped onto the table and spread his hands wide to keep his balance. He chanted . . .

> *"The boy stood on the burning deck,*
> *Picking his nose like crazy.*
> *He rolled them into little balls*
> *And flicked them till he felt hazy."*

The mob cheered. Even the gentleman writer smiled quietly at his writing paper. But Uncle Edward was annoyed. Getting annoyed was his b-i-g mistake, as you will see . . .

Twenty-two

The Storm Inn and the station

I am sorry that I had to upset your dinner with that disgusting poem. But sometimes life is like that, and sometimes people can be very rude. The real poem was written by a lady and is much more polite. She would be very upset if she knew what people have done to her famous poem. So (if you see her), don't tell her.

Uncle Edward filled his lungs with air and used his powerful voice to shout over the man on the table. The magic lantern flickered into life and showed the deck of a fine man-of-war ship. It rocked up and down as if it was riding the ocean waves.

The crowd settled down a little.

Then I pressed the switch that sent a small wheel spinning in the warm air from the lamp. The wheel held pieces of red and yellow glass. As they spun, they cast flickering flames onto the picture. It looked as if the warship was on fire.

The crowd was really hooked now. It should have been so easy. All we had to do was recite the poem as I acted out the part of the brave little boy. Then we could pack up and get to the station. It started off well enough. Uncle Edward boomed . . .

> *"The boy stood on the burning deck*
> *Whence all but he had fled;*
> *The flame that lit the battle's wreck,*
> *Shone round him o'er the dead."*

I stood between the lantern and the screen so that the "flames" ran across me, and I pretended to feel the heat. I heard someone sigh, "Ahhhh!" and I knew that my acting was breaking their hard hearts.

Uncle continued . . .

> *"Yet beautiful and bright he stood,*
> *As born to rule the storm;*
> *A creature of heroic blood,*
> *A proud, though childlike form."*

I looked proud (but childlike) in my sailor's uniform but still a little afraid of the flames.

> *"The flames roll'd on—he would not go*
> *Without his father's word;*
> *That father, faint in death below,*
> *His voice no longer heard."*

> *"He called aloud—"*

Now it was my turn to call out—and hope that I didn't forget the words . . .

> *"'Say, Father, say*
> *If yet my task is done?'"*

Uncle took up the terrible tale . . .

> *"He knew not that the chieftain lay*
> *Unconscious of his son."*

We picked up the pace as I continued in a panic:

"'Speak, Father!' once again he cried,
'If I may yet be gone!'"

Uncle rattled an iron sheet that sounded like the thunder of cannons and cried:

"And but the booming shots replied,
And fast the flames roll'd on."

The audience was on the edges of their seats. Then an awful woman stood on the table next to the man with the beard and glass eye. Suddenly, she cackled and screeched:

"The boy stood on the burning deck;
His feet were full of blisters.
The flames came up and burned his pants,
And now he wears his sister's!"

Now, I'd seen this happen before. One of two things would happen next—the crowd would choose. They would choose to support us, or they would choose to support the troublemaker. It all depended on what Uncle Edward did next.

He looked at the man with the beard. "Is that a wart on your arm, or is it your wife?"

One or two in the crowd giggled, but the joke didn't go down too well. The man with the beard was annoyed. "You can't talk about my lovely wife like that!" he shouted.

"Your lovely wife?" Uncle Edward jeered. "I've seen better faces on pirate flags. I've seen potatoes with prettier eyes."

The crowd was quiet. They were turning against us. NOW was the time for us to quit. But Uncle Edward was fired up. "Still, I don't suppose someone as ugly as *you* could get a better-looking woman!"

"Ugly?" the man cried.

"Yes! Is that really your face? Or did your neck just throw up?"

No one laughed. Still, Uncle Edward didn't see how it was all going wrong. "Why don't you just stick your nose in your ear and blow out your brains?" he teased.

The crowd muttered and began to boo. The man with the beard tried to step forward to attack Uncle Edward, but he forgot that he was standing on a table. He crashed down onto the table next to him.

A woman in a red satin dress screamed, "Hey! Your

glass eye just fell in my stew." She turned to the unshaven, square-jawed man next to her. "Harry! His glass eye fell in my stew. DO something!"

Harry wasn't sure if she wanted him to throw the one-eyed man off the table or get the glass eye out of her stew. He picked up the bearded man by the collar and the seat of his pants and threw him across the room. The one-eyed man landed on a card table and scattered the playing cards and money on the floor.

Some folks scrambled for the cash. The gamblers charged across the room at the square-jawed man, kicking tables and customers out of their way.

Soon everyone, except the gentleman writer in his corner, had gotten their beer or their stew spilled and was looking to get their revenge on someone. Punches were thrown. Then mugs were thrown. Finally, chairs were being thrown, and everyone was punching anyone within reach.

"Where was I?" Uncle Edward asked. He cleared his throat . . .

> *"And but the booming shots replied,*
> *And fast the flames roll'd on."*

No one was listening. I turned off the magic lantern and shouted to Theus, who was watching from the side of the stage, "Grab the coffin, Theus! Let's get to the station as fast as we can."

Theus understood. He picked up the coffin and placed it on his shoulder while I wrapped the magic lantern in the screen cloth and tugged on Uncle's arm.

"Time to go," I said.

Theus looked at the riot and muttered, "Where did I go wrong?"

"Theus, come ON!" I shouted.

He followed us out of the backstage door and into the cool, dark back alley. Uncle Edward was a little dazed. "I thought they liked us," he said.

"To the station, Uncle. The midnight train."

"Ah, yes," he said and fell into step with us.

Rats scuttled out of our way, and even the cutthroats in the shadows kept away from us. We stayed off the main streets, slithered over a lot of cobbles, and paddled through a lot of puddles. But before 11 chimed on the town hall clock, we had reached the station.

We bought our tickets with some of the money

from the coffin and then used it to sit on.

"Are you coming with us?" Uncle Edward asked Theus.

"I can't," the Titan said. "I had to leave my wings behind. I need to get them when the Storm Inn is a little quieter. Anyway, I have to stay and find a hero."

"You saw little Jim in the show tonight. That's a hero for you!" Uncle Edward argued.

"But that was just a myth," Theus said.

"No, no!" Uncle Edward cried. "It was a true story." [39]

Theus shook his head. "There is a temple in Eden City. I have to get back to it and find the hero himself. It's a quest that I have to do for my cousin."

"You've been a good help, my boy. I am getting too old to carry that coffin around much longer. We need a strong young man like you to help us out. Why not join us?" he asked cheerfully.

Then, from the shadows of the waiting room

39 Now, strange as it seems, Uncle was telling the truth (for a change). The boy who stood on the burning deck was an admiral's son, and the ship was called the *Orient*. The *Orient* was sunk, and the admiral's son waited for his father to let him go. His father couldn't—because he was dead. The boy was blown up with the ship. Look it up in a history book if you don't believe me!

doorway, a voice said, "He won't want to join you when he finds out that you are headed for a noose, Mr. Slaughter."

TWENTY-THREE

THE JAILHOUSE OF EDEN CITY

Just when you thought that we were going to get away with our loot, we were spotted at the station. Who in the world could it be? Had Mr. Mucklethrift tracked us down? Or had his butler noticed a missing mantel clock and guessed that we were the culprits? Take a guess. Which of the two?

A man stepped from the shadows. A weedy man with a weedy grin on his weedy face.

Uncle Edward jumped to his feet. "Mayor Tweed, my good and dear old friend!" he cried. "How wonderful to see you."

Tweed snapped his fingers, and Sergeant Sergeant stepped out of the dark waiting room. Two fat officers stood at his shoulder and blocked our escape. We were trapped like elephants in quicksand. If Uncle Edward was ever going to talk our necks out of nooses, this was the moment.

"Surely we don't need the police here," Uncle Edward said with a smile. "We don't want them to know about our little arrangement, do we?"

Tweed narrowed his eyes. "We had no arrangement, Slaughter."

Sergeant Sergeant looked a little confused. "Sorry, Mr. Mayor, what is he talking about?"

Tweed lied as easily as my uncle. "Oh, I pretended I would meet him to divvy up the spoils. In fact, I only wanted to make sure that he was caught red-handed with the loot. It's in the coffin."

"We agreed to share it," Uncle Edward said carefully. "I suppose we have to give the police a cut now, do we?"

Sergeant Sergeant sprang forward, his mustache quivering. "Bribe the police? Is that what you are trying to do? I canNOT be bribed! Not never, not ever!"

Uncle Edward shrugged. "Then arrest Mayor Tweed. He said he'd meet us at the Lost Duck to get his share."

"I went to find the Lost Duck a little early—and found that there was no such place," the mayor said.

Uncle Edward nodded. "And that's when you

decided to rat on us to the police, eh, Mayor Tweed?"

The mayor nodded. "I had hoped to arrest you myself," he agreed. "But when I found that you'd lied to me, I went to Sergeant Sergeant for help in tracking you down."

"Ah! So how did the good sergeant know that we were catching the midnight train?" Uncle Edward asked, puzzled.

"I told him," Theus said softly.

"What?" I said. "You betrayed us?"

Theus nodded miserably. "Remember? In the alley that leads to the Temple of the Hero? I said to him, 'I can't come back in the morning anyway. I'm taking the midnight train.' I didn't think it was important. But, yes, Jim. I betrayed you. I am sorry."

Mayor Tweed looked savage. "Sergeant! Lock them up and call the judge. I want to see them hang at dawn. All in a neat row outside the jailhouse. Take them away!"

"What about the loot, sir?" Sergeant Sergeant asked.

"Don't worry about that . . . I'll take care of it," the weaselly mayor promised, and his eyes glittered like the gold inside the box. "Make sure that these villains are secure. They are wanted in ten cities at least. The reward will be huge. Don't let them escape."

"No, sir." Sergeant Sergeant nodded to his two officers. "Officer Drab! Officer Dross! Secure the prisoners."

The police officers quickly threw chains around us. Theus gave a bitter laugh as we were led outside by the police. "I'm used to wearing chains."

"Ah, yes, you spent two hundred days in jail, didn't you?" Uncle Edward said as the horses started moving and we clattered down the road to death.

"Two hundred years, it was," Theus said quietly.

"You may be used to wearing chains," Sergeant Sergeant said, "but you sure ain't used to dying."

Theus managed a weak smile. "At least seventy thousand times," he said.

Sergeant Sergeant looked at Theus as if he was insane and shifted away from him.

But I wasn't interested. All I was worried about was how it would feel to die. I even felt spiteful toward Theus—at least he had practiced dying 70,000 times. And *he* was sure to come back to life. I wasn't a Titan with the power to fix my broken neck.[40]

40 Yes, YOU know that if Theus died, then he would give off a green spark. The Fury would spot it, hunt him down, and destroy him (*cont.*)

At last, the cart pulled up at the back of the jailhouse. I looked out at the free world one last time before I was led inside. In the distance I heard the train whistle blow. We had been so close to getting on that train, rich and free. So very close.[41]

We were thrown into the same cell together. The chains were left on our wrists.

"Hello, my friends!" someone cried from a bench against the wall. It was the blind beggar. "Imagine seeing you again!"

"I thought that you couldn't see us at all," I said.

"Ha! You never believed that for a minute, did you?"

"Not really," I said.

"I did," Theus said.

The beggar said, "Sergeant Sergeant walked past me and dropped a coin on the ground. Of course, I reached out and grabbed it. 'Oh, no!' he cried. 'You're no more a blind beggar than I am!' He arrested me and threw me in here. I guess I'll get a beating and be

40 (cont.) forever. Theus knew that. I didn't. When you are headed for the scaffold, you do NOT feel very kind toward the people around you. In that police cart I hated everyone.

41 Yes. All right. So I was feeling very sorry for myself. It's easy for you, sitting there waiting to see me get what I deserve. But I'll bet that YOU'LL feel pretty sorry for yourself when your time comes. Just you wait and see.

thrown out of town. Still, there's always another day, another town. What about you?"

"Robbery," Theus said.

"Ohhhh! No one important, I hope!"

"Mr. Mucklethrift of Mucklethrift Manor," I said.

The beggar's mouth fell open. "Oh, well, in that case, you have NO chance. Old Mucklethrift will demand to see you hang. See, you should have robbed someone poor like me. No problem. But get caught robbing the RICH, and . . . well, they just want revenge. They want an example made out of you. Sorry, fellers. Your ship has sunk. He'll probably drag the judge out of bed to try you tonight and hang you in the morning."

Uncle Edward looked at the beggar with a cold stare. "Be quiet, man. Think of young Jim. An old villain like me deserves to die. But Jim here is an innocent—he only did what I told him to do. He only did it to survive. He doesn't deserve to die."

The beggar looked at his filthy feet. "Sorry, I wasn't thinking," he mumbled.

"Not as sorry as I am," Uncle Edward sighed. He looked at me, and for the first time in his life he wasn't acting. "I am so sorry, Jim. If they said I could die and you could live, then I'd let them hang me and be happy."

"Maybe there's a way that we can all be happy," Theus said brightly. "There is a way."

We turned and looked at him.

"You've thought of a way? You have a plan?" I asked.

"No, there IS a way . . . I just don't know what it is."

"Thanks, Theus," I said. "You are a great comfort."

The keys rattled in the lock, and the jailer looked in. "The judge is ready for you now," he said.

TWENTY-FOUR

THE COURTHOUSE IN EDEN CITY

Yes, it's another cliff-hanger. "How will Jim get out of this one?" you ask. It's like Theus said—there IS a way, but we just couldn't see it at the time. Looking back now, it seems so simple. What we needed was a writer to solve the problem. But in those days I wasn't a writer. I was just a very scared little boy.

The judge had very white hair and a very red face. He looked annoyed. That was not a good sign.

"This court is in session," he said quickly. "You are brought to trial before me, Judge Jasper Coot."

A few people had drifted in off the street to see the late-night show. We'd done dozens of performances, but this was going to be our most important. There was an area at the back of the court where the public sat. The door opened, and I saw a red-haired girl tiptoe in holding the hand of a bearded man with a fountain pen. Word of our trial had spread quickly through the slippery streets. January Storm had come to see me die. I hoped that it would make her happy.

But she didn't look happy. Neither did the gentleman writer. She sat there with her face as pale as the Eden City fog and clutched a grubby handkerchief to her mouth. Her dark eyes followed every character in the drama that we were acting out.

We gave our names. The judge scowled when Theus said, "Prometheus Titan," and then he started to speak quickly in a whining tone.

"Tonight I was at a wonderful party given by my dear friend George Mucklethrift. Not only was my poor old friend cruelly robbed of his hard-earned wealth, but I was dragged away from that party to judge you villains. Then I discovered that some money was missing from my wallet. I am not a happy judge," he said.

I knew that I had seen him before. A few hours ago he'd been one of the guests at Mucklethrift Manor, and he'd been clapping loudly after we had performed

"The Uncle."

The judge rapped his wooden gavel on the bench in front of him, sipped some water, and went on, "In ancient Greece there was a judge named Draco—"

"I knew him," Theus said, nodding.

The judge scowled at the Titan. "Do not make fun of this court, young man. I will punish you until you wish that you had never set eyes on me. Now, where was I?"

"Draco," Sergeant Sergeant reminded him, and his boiled gooseberry eyes were turned toward Judge Jasper Coot.

"Ah, yes, Draco. This Draco said he could punish criminals by executing them. But thievery was such a horrible crime that he wished he could think of a punishment WORSE than execution."[42] The judge waved his gavel at us and said, "I know how Draco felt. But the worst I can do to you three is to have you hanged at dawn in front of the courthouse so that the good people of Eden City can see what happens to

---

42   This sounds like a pretty stupid thing to say. It just happens to be true. Draco really did live in ancient Greece, and he really was the cruelest judge on Earth—even crueler than Judge Jasper Coot, as you will see.

rogues like you. Take them away, Sergeant Sergeant, and have the scaffold ready when eight o'clock strikes."

The policeman rose to his feet and spoke quietly. "Sorry, Judge Coot, but I really can't do that."

"Can't? Can't? You must obey an Eden City judge, or you will hang alongside these evil men. Why *can't* you take them away and hang them?" the angry judge demanded.

"Because, your honor, they haven't had a trial," Sergeant Sergeant reminded him.

The judge smashed his gavel down on the bench and said, "Oh, very well. Seems like a waste of time to me, but let's get on with it as quickly as possible."

He turned to us with a look of disgust. "You are charged with robbing the home of Mr. George Mucklethrift—how do you plead?"

"Not guilty," Theus said.

The judge looked at the ceiling. "Look, young man, if you plead 'not guilty,' then we have to hear your case, get witnesses in, gather evidence—that all takes time. Then we'll hang you in the morning anyway. It's easier for all of us if you just say 'guilty,' understand?"

"Yes, your honor."

"You mean 'yes' you are guilty?"

"No, I am not," Theus said.

The judge glared at him for a minute. Theus looked back at him calmly. The judge turned to me. "So, are you guilty, sonny?"

"Not guilty," I said. From the back of the court, January gave a small cheer.

The judge banged his gavel in anger. "Silence in the court. Any repeat of that, and I will have you thrown out." He turned to Uncle Edward. "Surely YOU aren't going to tell me that you are not guilty?"

Uncle Edward looked very noble as he stood there, chin stuck out, head held high. "I could save you a lot of time, your honor."

"You could?"

"I could plead guilty," he offered.

The judge leaned forward. "I'd still have to hear all of the evidence against your two friends," he said. "You won't be saving me much time."

"What I thought was this," Uncle Edward said in a cheerful voice, as if he was talking to an old friend. "You let these two youngsters go, I plead guilty, you sentence me to . . . a sentence, and then we can all get to bed."

The judge leaned back and half closed his eyes to think about it. "Why would I want to let two criminals loose on the streets of Eden City? It's my job to keep the streets clean of vermin like them."

"Well," Uncle Edward said calmly. "You could set them free but throw them out of Eden City. Banish them. If they come back within five years, they'll hang."

The judge looked at Uncle Edward with some respect. "That's a good idea, old man. You should be a lawyer!"

"I used to be," Uncle Edward said. "That's what makes me such a good thief."[43]

"And you think I should let these two go?"

"You have to," Uncle Edward said. "Theus here knew nothing about the plot to rob the good Mr. Mucklethrift. He was just some poor young man who I met in the Storm Inn. He looked strong enough to carry the loot away, so I invited him

43 That was the first time I'd heard of Uncle Edward being a lawyer. I never did find out if this was the truth or if Uncle Edward had made it up. But he had a point—the most dishonest person in Eden City was probably Judge Jasper Coot, not Uncle Edward.

along. But you won't find a penny of the loot in his pockets, and he had no idea that he was taking part in a crime."

The judge nodded. He smacked the gavel on the bench and ordered, "Set Prisoner Prometheus Titan free, Sergeant."

Officer Drab (or it could have been Officer Dross) unlocked the chains, and Theus stepped down from the platform. He wandered to the back of the court, where January shuffled up her seat to make room for him. The judge turned his red-rimmed eyes on me. "But this boy *is* part of the plot. You are known all over the country for your little scheme. This Jim explores the house before the robbery. Then he steals the loot while you keep the master of the house busy. Don't tell me that Jim is innocent?"

My uncle placed a hand on my shoulder. "Jim is guilty," he said.

January gave a small cry. "Thanks, Uncle," I muttered.

Somehow Uncle Edward changed from being the judge's friend to being an actor on a stage. I knew the signs—the way he held himself, the way he used his voice. Uncle Edward was about to give the last great performance of his life in order to save a life. But he wasn't hoping to save his own life—he could see it was too late for that. He was saving mine.

"Judge Coot," he said. His voice was soft, yet it carried all around the oak walls of the courtroom. You could have heard a pin drop.[44] "Jim is guilty. I do not expect you to change the great laws of Eden City to set him free to rob again. What I do ask is that you use that finest of human feelings . . . mercy. For, when we use mercy, it drops like rain from heaven upon the ground below."

"I've heard that somewhere before," the judge agreed.

"Little Jim was in an orphanage when I found him. A harmless, helpless, motherless child whose life was in danger."

"Mortal danger?"

"He was starved and beaten and made to work at weaving machines till he dropped," Uncle Edward said.

---

44 That's what people say, of course. What I MEAN is that I didn't hear a pin drop. This could have been because I was wrong—you couldn't hear a pin drop. Or it might have meant that no one actually dropped a pin in that court. I guess I'll never know. I do not plan to go back to the court and start dropping pins to find out if you can hear them. Sorry, keep reading.

"That's what homeless children are for; that's how Mucklethrift makes his money, using children like that," the judge argued.

A faint red spot of anger appeared on Uncle Edward's cheek. He wanted to shout, "Then Mucklethrift is a monster!" But he swallowed his anger and went on.

"This poor child," he said, patting my shoulder, "faced something worse than death at the weaving looms. He was taken from the orphanage by a common criminal named Edward Slaughter. He faced death at the end of a rope if he was caught."

"That's worse," the judge agreed.

"Little Jim was like the boy who stood on the burning deck. Jim pleaded to be set free from his duties," Uncle Edward said, and his voice was breaking with the pain of the tale. "Every night he sobbed himself to sleep. Every night he pleaded, 'Uncle Edward, Uncle Edward, can I stop now?'"

"I did that?" I asked.

Uncle Edward tightened his grip on my shoulder till it hurt. It was a sign for me to keep quiet. Then he raised his voice and lifted his free hand to the candle chandelier as if *he* was the pleading boy.

He stole the lines from the poem—well, it was the last thing that he'd ever steal—and he cried in a childlike voice:

> "'Say, Uncle, say
> If yet my task is done?
> Speak, Uncle!' once again he cried,
> 'If I may yet be gone!'"

Someone in the public area sobbed. January bit hard into her handkerchief. The judge sniffed.

"You turned down this poor child's plea?" the judge asked.

"I did. That's why I deserve to die *twice*, and the boy deserves to live," Uncle Edward explained.

The judge wiped a tear from his eye. "Sergeant, take this man away. Hang him in the morning."

"Yes, Judge Coot. And what about the boy?"

"Set him free. Send him back to his orphanage on the ten o'clock train tomorrow morning."

Officer Dross (or it could have been Officer Drab) unfastened my chains.

There was a lot of noise in the court as the judge rose and left. But one voice was screaming louder

than all the rest. It was screaming, "No! Please, no!"
I realized that the pitiful voice was mine.

TWENTY-FIVE

EDEN CITY, THE MORNING OF THE EXECUTION

Well, that looks like it, doesn't it? That's how I came to be telling the story. Uncle Edward was hanged, while I lived. Theus was free to escape. End of story—happy ending for me. Unhappy ending for my uncle. But life is never that simple. If you were planning to close the book, turn off the light, and go to sleep, then go ahead. But I have to warn you—you will be missing a few twists in my tale . . .

The Fury was floating over Earth on its huge wings and letting time hurry by. Below, it could see a stream of blue flashes as human spirits fled from their bodies. From time to time there would be a war, and a corner of Earth would be awash with blue light.

The Avenger shook its head on its crooked neck—

why were these pitiful humans so stupid? Pandora had brought them enough plagues and diseases to kill them in their millions. Why would they want to help the vengeful gods by killing each other? The Fury would never understand the little hairless beasts.

Time sped by, and bright Earth turned more drab, even on the sunlit side. The Fury found it hard to see some parts of the land now. Huge cities smothered themselves in blankets of smoke. Factory chimneys belched out stinking clouds of the stuff, hiding the hovels in the squalid streets below.

But the smoke didn't hide the blue sparks of death. And these cities glowed as blue as battlefields; crushing machines crashed down on workers, and then the foul and fetid water finished off the widows and children. The smoke charred children's lungs. Empty plates and emptier bellies sent the weakest wearily into the gutters to splutter out like fading candles.

Another blue spark here and one hundred more there.

One city was more muddied and puddled than all the rest. The Fury tried to close its nostrils as it drifted down through the soiled air to see what misery lay below. In the heart of this stained city there was one particular blackened chimney that choked the atmosphere more than all the rest, and even more blue flashes appeared from this particular factory.

But this city felt "right" to the Fury. If this city was a creature, it would have been the sort of creature that would rip out your liver as soon as it looked at you. Yes, it was a city that was as vicious and ugly as a spider, as cruel and cunning as a cat—but it felt "right."

The Fury landed on an arch above the gateway and watched, like some hungry vulture, as another lifeless human was carried from the building in a faded blanket.

There were strange symbols painted on the arch. The Fury couldn't read them. Otherwise it would have known that they were words spelling out "Mucklethrift's Machines."

A little match girl on the corner looked up at the hideous bird and shuddered. She picked up a clump of mud from the gutter and threw it.

The Fury turned its crooked neck and fixed a cruel eye on her. It could almost see the blue flash quivering, ready to be set free. "You'll soon be dead," it creaked.

It spread its monstrous wings and flapped slowly into the air. "If this is what the humans did with Prometheus's foolish gift, he deserves his fate," the bird thought. It rose above the sooty air and went on with its search. It didn't know how close it had come.

Nor did it see a winged horse flying high up above it.

Zeus sat astride the magical creature and reined it in. "Whoa, Pegasus. We don't want the Fury to see us. If it spots us, it will follow us all the way to cousin Theus."

The god turned the creature's head and flew out to the dark side of the Moon to hide for a while. That's how Zeus missed the execution.

I wish I could have missed it.

★★★

The scaffold was high, but I struggled to see it. I stood on the coffin that we'd brought from the Storm Inn, but I still wasn't tall enough to see. There were too many people crowded in front of the wooden platform. "Uncle Edward always loved a high stage and a big audience," I thought sadly.

I was stuck behind the fat figure of Mr. George Mucklethrift. He stood between his friends, Judge Coot and Mayor Tweed. This hanging was going to be a good start to the day for them.

The whole mood of the crowd made it feel like some sort of party. A breakfast party. They had come to see a man die and then go home to their coffee.

January Storm stood silent at my left side. The gentleman writer also stood on the left, stroking his beard. "The days of hanging people in public should be long gone," he said. "If a man has to die, let him die in peace and dignity," he said.

The three great men of Eden City chatted happily. "A great day for Eden City," Mr. Mucklethrift said with a chuckle. "You did a good job there, Mayor Tweed, trapping this villainous Edward Slaughter. He is wanted all over the country, yet he has slipped through the hands of the law everywhere else."

"I knew he was a fiend as soon as I set eyes on him," Tweed boasted. "There is an old saying, 'Give a man enough rope, and he will hang himself.' Well, I gave him enough time, and he betrayed his wicked plans."

Mr. Mucklethrift laughed. "But he's not going to

hang himself, is he? Sergeant Sergeant is going to hang him! Ha!"

Tweed giggled. He looked up to the white-haired judge. "It would have been good to see the three of them hanging side by side," he sighed.

The judge shook his head. "The young man was a handsome creature. People don't like to see beauty destroyed. The mob might have turned against us."

"We wouldn't want that," Mr. Mucklethrift said, suddenly serious. "I heard what they did at the Storm Inn last night. We have to keep them happy with a hanging or two—but we don't want to make them angry—oh, no."

"That's why I let the little boy go free," the judge continued. "The mob would have felt pity for his feeble frame dangling there. They have soft hearts where children are concerned."

"Even thieving little devils like that one?" Mr. Mucklethrift sneered.

"Trust me, George," the judge said. "The boy would be too light to hang."

"Not like Slaughter, eh? He's as fat as butter, that one," Mayor Tweed said.

"Anyway, you got your valuables back, didn't you?" the judge asked.

Mr. Mucklethrift grumbled, "Only half of them—the rest must be hidden away or has already been spent."

Mayor Tweed shuffled his weedy feet. I knew where the missing loot had gone. But it was none of my business if friends robbed friends.

The fog had lifted a little, and the sun was rising like a crimson ball over the river. The sky was flooded with a dull red light. It looked stained with the blood of all the humans who had died in that cruel city.

The crowd fell suddenly silent. Two things had happened. The town hall clock had begun its chime for the dying hour. *Ding-dong, ding-dong.* And a gate in the jailhouse wall had opened.

Ding-dong, ding-dong. Every chime struck another second off the life of a man. He climbed the steps slowly, head down. His hands were tied behind him.

Ding-dong, ding-dong.

He stopped at the top of the platform. His head stayed down, but his eyes glanced up and looked into mine.

Ding-dong, ding-dong.

One eye closed slowly in a wink that no one saw but me and January.

Donnnngggg!

The first stroke of his last hour chimed.

Donnnngggg!

He raised his head a little, and his big eyes glowed in gray shadows of greasepaint.

Donnnngggg!

He took out a piece of paper and began to read . . .

Donnnngggg!

"It is a far, far better thing that I do than I have ever done," he said.

Donnnngggg!

Sergeant Sergeant slipped a noose around his neck.

Donnnngggg!

"It is a far, far better rest that I go to than I have ever known," the condemned man concluded.

The gentleman writer murmured, "Well said."

Donnnngggg!

Sergeant Sergeant placed a white hood over his victim's head.

Donnnngggg!

The last bell rang like doom. Sergeant Sergeant stepped back and pulled a lever. The floor of the scaffold opened, and the fat figure fell through.

There was a gasp from the mob. Somehow I'd expected a cheer. But those noble words had made them silent and thoughtful.[45] They began to shuffle off, a little ashamed. January gave a low moan, and the gentleman writer let out a deep groan. Only the three great men of Eden City looked happy.

"What was all that about far, far better things?" Mr. Mucklethrift asked.

"I don't know," Mayor Tweed said with a shrug. "But I thought it sounded quite nice."

"Nothing 'nice' about being hanged for theft," Judge Coot grumbled.

"A far, far better rest?" Mr. Mucklethrift said, scratching his head.

"We'll all have a better rest tonight, knowing that fat fiend is out of our way," the judge sniffed.

Mr. Mucklethrift slapped them both on the back. "And we will all enjoy a better breakfast this

45 If you think that you've heard those words before, it could be that you have. The gentleman writer used them at the end of a famous book that he wrote in 1859, one year after this hanging. But the words were first spoken, in real life, on that scaffold in Eden City. I don't mind the gentleman writer using the words, of course. After all, he had drafted them for the doomed man's speech, hadn't he?

morning, my friends. Come back to Mucklethrift Manor and join me," he said and guided them through the thinning crowd.

They left without a glance back at the scaffold. But we three stayed. We had work to do. We picked up the coffin—January and I at the bottom and the gentleman writer at the head.

Sergeant Sergeant's two big police officers were laying the lifeless shape on the cold cobbles behind the scaffold. The scaffold was one of those Eden City shadows that was blacker than a bottle of ink, staining the air around it. We dragged the coffin out of the shadow, yet some of the shadow seemed to cling to it. I pressed the switch to open the lid.

Nothing happened.

I gave it a kick, and the lid flew open. I really *would* have to fix that switch one day. No skeleton named Skinny popped up. We'd left Skinny in a corner of the stage at the Storm Inn. "Can you help us put Uncle into the coffin?" I asked Officer Drab.

They looked at one another. "We are supposed to bury him inside the jailhouse walls," Officer Dross said.

"Have you dug the grave?" I asked.

"We haven't had time. It's taken us all night to set up the scaffold," Officer Drab complained.

"So," the gentleman writer said, "you won't want to start digging through cold clay now, will you?"

"Why . . . no . . ."

"So, let us take the body away and give it a respectable burial."

"I suppose . . ."

"That way the boy will be able to visit the grave with flowers every day," the gentleman writer said.

"He's due to get on the ten o'clock train," Officer Dross reminded us.

"I'll put the flowers there for you, poor little Jim," January offered. "Don't cry."

"I wasn't crying."

"Well, you *should* be . . . you've just watched your dear old uncle hang!" she snapped.

"Oh, yes! Boo! Hoo! Oh, poor old Uncle! Waaaah!"

"Yes, all right!" Officer Dross said. "Here, look, we'll tuck your uncle away nice and comfy in his coffin . . . just stop wailing."

I stopped.

"Now, make sure he gets a proper burial," Officer

Dross said to the gentleman writer.

"I will."

Officer Drab patted me on the head and walked off.

"Time for breakfast," Officer Dross said.

"We've earned it for a good morning's work," Officer Drab agreed.

The gentleman writer, January, and I struggled to pick up the loaded coffin. But once we were moving, we got into a rhythm and trotted through the red-washed streets—as red as blood from a freshly torn liver—to the Storm Inn.

We placed the coffin carefully on the stage. I pushed the switch. Nothing happened.

Then a tubby figure stepped from behind the curtain. He was dressed in a green coat, and he wore a worried frown. He raised a boot and kicked the switch.

The lid flew open.

The figure in the green coat knelt by the coffin. "Theus, my boy? How are you feeling?"

The corpse opened its eyes and groaned. "My throat hurts," he croaked and sat up stiffly. He rose to his feet a little shakily.

Uncle Edward took a handkerchief out of the pocket of his green coat and mopped his brow. "I owe you my life, young Theus. Thank the Lord that you are alive."

Theus and Uncle Edward wrapped their arms around each other.

I wrapped my arms around January Storm. The gentleman writer looked on and smiled.

TWENTY-SIX

THE STORM INN, THE NIGHT BEFORE THE EXECUTION

A terrible thing has happened. As I was writing this record, I somehow shuffled the papers, and this chapter got out of order. Oh, dear. Look, let's go back a little way to the trial. We were in the courtroom. Uncle Edward was sentenced to hang, and I cried out, "No! Please, no!"—remember? After the trial, THIS happened. It will help explain some of the last chapter. Sorry about that. I hope it doesn't spoil your enjoyment. I'll try not to do it again.

They tell me that I fainted. They say Theus picked me up and carried me back to the Storm Inn. All I know is that I woke up on the stage. My head was resting on the magic lantern that was covered in the white cloth.

Theus had placed his wings over me to keep me warm.

I opened my eyes. The room was not how we'd left it. There was hardly a table or chair that hadn't been smashed and splintered. The gentleman writer, Theus, and January sat on the coffin in a row like three gloomy crows on a rooftop.

It was an almost empty coffin now. The police had emptied it of the loot and left Skinny the skeleton chipped and cracked and pathetic looking.

January didn't look like her sharp-faced, ugly self any longer. Her eyes were red from crying, and her nose was red from sniffling. "Are you all right, Jim?" she asked.

"No," I said. "Uncle Edward will die, and I'll be thrown out of Eden City. I've got nowhere to go. If they try to send me back to the orphanage, I'll run away."

"You'll starve," the gentleman writer said.

"I don't care," I said, and I think I sounded as bleak as the foghorn on the river outside. "I wish I could hang alongside Uncle Edward. At least it would be a quick end."

"No," Theus said. "It was my fault. If I hadn't

gone looking for the Temple of the Hero, I wouldn't have told the sergeant where to find us. We'd have been on that train and a hundred miles away from here."

I sighed. "Uncle Edward gave his life to save mine," I said. "I always thought that he never cared. I never thought that he could be so . . ."

"Noble," the gentleman writer said, giving me one of his fine writer's words.

"Noble," I agreed and sat up.

"A hero," January said.

"A what?" Theus asked suddenly.

"A hero," she repeated.

"Then I have to save him," Theus said. "I have to show him to Zeus."

"Who?" the gentleman writer asked.

"My . . . cousin," Theus said. He had told me most of his story but didn't want to waste time telling the other two.

"You can't save him," January argued. "No one ever escapes from Eden City Jailhouse."

Theus rose from the coffin. "It was my fault," he repeated. "I should be hanging instead of him."

"But then YOU'D be dead," January argued.

"What good would that do?"

"But what if I *lived*?" Theus asked.

I knew what he meant, but the gentleman writer shook his head. "Impossible."

"No, it's not," January said, jumping to her feet. "I've heard about this before. There IS a way to cheat the rope."

We looked at her as she jumped up onto the coffin. She acted out putting a rope around her neck. "The rope pulls your throat closed and chokes you," she said. "But I have heard that some victims put a strong metal tube down their throat. It saves them. Their friends take the body for burial, pull out the tube, and wake the person up."

"Yes!" the gentleman writer cried. "An English highwayman did it a hundred years ago, I think. It worked for him."

"So, all we have to do is smuggle in a piece of pipe to Mr. Slaughter," January said.

I shook my head. "I'll bet that highwayman was a healthy young man. Uncle Edward is old and fat. The drop would kill him."

Theus nodded. "That's why we need a young man to take his place."

"I can't do it," I sighed. "I'd like to, but it wouldn't work."

"That's why I have to be the one," Theus said eagerly.

January Storm shook her head. "Sorry, but I don't see how you can take the place of a fat old man."

"I do!" Theus cried. "Remember, in Mucklethrift Manor, Uncle Edward said, 'I need to make myself look like a horrible fat old man.' And I told him he *was* a horrible fat old man. But he put that paint on his face . . ."

"Greasepaint," I said.

"Yes . . . and powder in his hair. Well, *I* could do that," Theus said.

"You can't just jump on the scaffold, knock Mr. Slaughter out of the way, and take his place," January argued.

"Ha!" the gentleman writer cried. "I have the answer. It's like the plot from a book. We dress Theus as Mr. Slaughter, and then we go to visit him in jail. We tell the guards that Theus is your uncle's twin brother."

I nodded. "When we get inside the cell, we leave Theus behind to hang—with the pipe down his throat—and walk out with the real Uncle Edward."

"Perfect," the gentleman writer said. "And it will make a perfect ending to the story I am writing this month."

"Theus will have to give a speech on the scaffold," January said. "They always do that."

"What do I say?" Theus asked, worried.

"Oh, I'll write something for you," the gentleman writer offered. "It's my job."

"Get dressed in Uncle Edward's spare clothes," I said to Theus and pointed to my uncle's bag on the side of the stage. My faintness was gone now, and the blood was bubbling in my brain. Uncle Edward had saved me from the orphanage, and now I could repay him and save him from the scaffold.[46]

The makeup box was safe beneath Skinny's crumbling skull. In just ten minutes I had made Theus look like Uncle Edward—at least he would pass for him in the faint candlelight of Eden City Jailhouse and in the foggy morning light.

46 Strangely, it never entered my mind that Uncle Edward had saved me from one horror—the orphanage—only to throw me into the worse horror of hanging. I never blamed him for that. All I wanted to do was save him.

Uncle Edward had been wearing his black coat. His spare coat was dark green. "They're not the same," January groaned. "The guard will spot the difference."

"No, no!" the gentleman writer said, grinning. "That makes it *better*. We switch coats inside the cell. A green coat walks in, and a green coat walks out— the guard will not be looking at the face. Just the coat."

"Of course," January agreed. "I'm a fool."

For just a moment, a flash of the old sarcasm sparked in me. "Yep. She went to a mind reader, but he gave her money back," I quipped.

She turned on me. "Go back to the country— some village is missing its idiot!"

"If you were twice as smart, you'd be a half-wit."

"If brains were gunpowder, you wouldn't have enough to blow off your hat."

"There's no time for this," the gentleman writer cried, stepping between us. "January, go and find us a piece of pipe that Theus can use."

She ran off into the kitchen. The gentleman writer shook his head. "This is the bravest thing I've ever seen," he said.

Theus shrugged. "It's nothing," he said, and he

caught my eye. We both knew that Theus would live on after they hung him. Then I remembered something. While the gentleman writer went to find some paper to write Theus's scaffold speech on, I whispered, "Theus . . . you'll be using godly powers."

"I know."

"There'll be a green spark, and the Fury will track you down."

"Yes."

"And this time you'll be destroyed forever. Ground into dust."

He nodded. "That's why you have to get me in the coffin, bring me back to the inn, and have my wings waiting for me. With any luck I'll be away before the Fury tracks me down."

"And without luck?"

He left the question hanging in the air . . . like a man on the end of a rope.

TWENTY-SEVEN

THE STORM INN, AFTER THE EXECUTION

Sorry about that. We are now back with my chapters in the right order. Theus was hanged instead of Uncle Edward— and then came back to life as only a Titan could. You will remember that we were all happy that Theus AND Uncle Edward had survived the execution. But our problems weren't over. We were hugging each other on the stage when we really should have been moving quickly to complete our escapes. Very quickly.

Hugging January Storm was something that I never thought I'd do. "You are so bony that it's like hugging Skinny the skeleton," I told her.

She hugged me harder. "Just what I was thinking when I was hugging you," she said and laughed. She didn't look half as ugly when she laughed.

The gentleman writer stroked his beard and said quietly, "You aren't safe yet, you know. Jim has to get on that ten o'clock train, or they'll come looking for him. And if they spot Mr. Slaughter still alive, they'll take him off and hang him again."

January let go of me and looked up at Theus. "The pipe in the throat worked then?" she asked.

Theus took the pipe from his pocket and showed it to her.

She frowned. "When did you take it out of your throat?" she asked.

"While I was lying in the coffin being carried along here," Theus lied.[47]

She nodded. "So how do we get Mr. Slaughter out of town?"

"In the coffin, I guess," I said.

January groaned. "It was all I could manage to carry Theus back here," she said, rubbing her skinny arms. "I'm not sure I could carry someone as fat . . .

---

47   That's right. You and I know that he never used the pipe trick. He simply let himself die. But January never knew that. It would have taken too much time to tell her the full story. We didn't have any time. And she may not have believed the story of Titans, gods, and Furies anyway. All that matters is that YOU believe it.

I mean, *great* as Mr. Slaughter."

Uncle Edward stood tall and sucked in his stomach. "I hate to weigh so heavily on my friends," he said. "I owe young Theus everything. Life and liberty, my boy. And yet, I find myself humbly begging for one more favor. Can you help these poor motherless children carry me to the station?"

Theus paused for just a moment.

"He can't!" I said. "He has to leave. He has to leave right now. Before it's too late."

"Too late for what?" January asked.

"Nothing," I muttered.

"Too late for nothing is too early for something," Uncle Edward said.

"Huh?" I blinked. "Look, Uncle, take my word for it. Theus doesn't have a moment to spare. He has his own problems."

Theus looked miserable and torn. Then he forced a smile and said, "No, I have time. Don't worry, Jim."

"Don't *worry*!" I cried.

"I want to see you safe before I leave," he said. "Don't argue. But let's be as quick as we can."

I shook my head, defeated. A human cannot beat a Titan.

January and the gentleman writer were already busy. They helped Uncle Edward climb into the coffin and then stuffed Skinny the skeleton alongside him. At his feet they found room for the makeup box and the magic lantern. The gentleman writer cut a hole in the lid of the coffin using a small pocketknife that he kept to clean his pipe. We slipped January's pipe—the one that she thought had saved the life of Theus—through the hole so Uncle Edward could breathe.

Theus picked up one end of the coffin and the gentleman writer the other. As we hurried down the street, people moved out of the way. Well, you wouldn't want to stand in the way of a coffin, would you?

Sergeant Sergeant was waiting for me at the station.

The town hall clock struck nine—one hour before my train was to leave.

The policeman handed me a ticket and another one for Theus.

I'd forgotten that Theus was supposed to leave town with me. But Theus didn't want to be trapped on a train when the Fury arrived. He wanted to be on his wings and far away.

We had to make sure that the sergeant left before the train pulled in. Time ticked by. The policeman sat on a platform bench to wait.

His gooseberry eyes spotted the pipe in the coffin lid. "You taking the old skeleton with you? You're not planning to go on with the act now that your uncle's dead, are you?"

"I may do it with Theus here," I said.

"So what's the pipe in the lid for?" the policeman asked.

"So the skeleton can get fresh air," I said.

"It breathes?"

"No . . . but it gets moldy if it's sealed up. Smells like rotting bones," I lied.

Sergeant Sergeant nodded and sat there.

I tugged January by the arm and pulled her toward the door of the waiting room. "I have to get rid of the policeman," I said.

"Why?"

"Theus can't get on the train. Can you help?" I pleaded.

"Can a girl outsmart a boy?" she asked.

"No," I said.

"Wrong answer, dummy," she said. "Yes, a girl *can*

218

outsmart a boy—so, yes, I can help. Watch me."

She ran quickly to the station entrance and vanished around the corner. A minute ticked by . . . another precious, dangerous minute. Then she appeared again, scampering and screaming through the entrance to the station. "Oh, Sergeant Sergeant!" she cried. "There's been a terrible accident down by the harbor!"

"By the harbor?"

"One of Mr. Mucklethrift's ships crashed into the pier."

"Anyone hurt?"

"No one was hurt—but Mr. Mucklethrift is desperate to have the ship unloaded before it sinks. He's offering gold to anyone who helps."

The gooseberry eyes were bulging. "It is my duty as an officer of the law to help in disasters like this. I would help the good Mr. Mucklethrift without a penny as a reward."

"I'm sure you would . . . but if you get there now, you'll get lots of pennies. You'll be rich. There are all sorts of street beggars heading for the scene—they'll get the money if you don't hurry," she burbled on.

Sergeant Sergeant looked at us. "I have to go. They

need a leader. A man in charge."

"So go," the gentleman writer said. "I'll make sure that these criminals get on the train," he offered.

"You are a true gentleman, sir," the policeman said, and he almost tripped over his club in his hurry to get to the reward.

January smiled. "There you are. It'll take him half an hour to get to the harbor. By the time he asks around and finds there's no accident, it'll be way past nine-thirty."

The platform clock ticked on to five past nine. "By the time he gets back here," she resumed, "the train will be gone, and he won't know who got on it."

"Well done, young January," Theus said, and she glowed with pride. He hugged her briefly and shook hands with the gentleman writer and then with me. "And thanks for helping me, Jim," he said.

"Just *go*!" I moaned. "Run! Get your wings from the Storm Inn and fly!"

"He can really fly?" January gasped.

Theus nodded his handsome head. "I need to make one last visit before I leave the city, and then I'll be gone. Good-bye—and good luck," he said.

Then he was gone. And that should have been the

last that I saw of the Titan.[48]

"But you'll be in trouble, young lady," the gentleman writer reminded her. "The sergeant could lock you up for that."

"He won't," January said with a grin, "because I won't be here when he gets back. I'll be on the train with Jim and Uncle Edward."

"You will?" I asked.

"Yes. I'm tired of slaving away at the Storm Inn—and you made sure it was wrecked last night anyway. Father won't miss me . . . and you two need a woman to take care of you."

"We've managed all right up till now," I said.

She placed her hands on her hips and looked at me. "You have lost all the loot you stole," she reminded me.

"True."

"You have been caught by the police."

"Yes, but . . ."

"You have been thrown out of the city . . ."

<hr>

48 But it wasn't, as you will see. However, I won't spoil the story for you by telling you when I saw him next. You have to remember that a writer's job is to keep you guessing and turning the pages. Haven't you learned ANYTHING from me? Now get back to the story.

"I know, but . . ."

"And Uncle Edward escaped death by a miracle."

"Yes, well . . ."

"Next time you may not be so lucky," she said. "And you know that a girl *can* outsmart a boy—so who better than a girl to go along with you?"

"You don't have a ticket!" I cried.

"I have the ticket that your friend Theus won't be using," she said, and her grin was sharper than the gentleman writer's pocketknife.

My mouth opened and closed, but the words to defeat her wouldn't find their way into my mouth.

"Give up, Jim," the gentleman writer advised.

"I give up," I said.

January turned on her heels. "I'm going home to the Storm Inn to pack a few things. I'll be back in time for the train," she said and ran off.

The clock ticked on to ten past nine.

"Sir? Will you look after Uncle Edward?" I asked the gentleman writer, nodding at the coffin.

"Of course. Why?"

"I have to see someone before I leave."

I left the station for one last trip into Eden City.

Twenty-eight

All around Eden City that morning

My story is like a snowball. The farther it goes, the faster it rolls. Scenes change and spin. Characters run in and out where before they walked. Try to stay with the snowball. There is not much farther for it to roll.

The red dawn sun had risen above the low Eden City haze and fog. The light turned to a dirty yellow. But above the haze the sky was clear, and you could have seen two pairs of wings up there—circling. One low and just above the clouds. The other high and just below the setting moon.

The lower pair belonged to a monstrous brown bird with a vicious beak and a cruel eye.

The other wings sprouted from the back of a white

horse. A god sat on top of it and watched the brown bird as it dived down into the filthy air of Eden City. The white horse followed. It dropped faster than a comet. It fell like . . . well, like a horse from the sky.[49]

★★★

I hurried through the crowded streets, past the beggars and the crossing sweeper. The match girl was slumped in a doorway. She looked pale and was too weak to cry out, "Matches for sale."

Uncle Edward's money was in her wallet, but she needed more than money now. She needed care and love.

I turned the corner by the jailhouse and stopped so suddenly that my feet skidded on the slimy street. I backed away around the corner and then peeked around it fearfully.

The police officers had finished their breakfast, and they were back. They had stopped dismantling the scaffold to talk to a stranger. This stranger seemed to be dressed from head to toe in a brown cloak.

---

49 I know you don't see many horses falling from the sky—in fact, you may not see any if you live for one million years. You can imagine it, can't you? You can't? I didn't see it myself. But I can imagine it, so why can't you?

A feathered cloak. His face was as harsh as a hawk's, and his nose was yellow, like a beak.

"You say a man died here this morning?" he was asking.

"Yes," Officer Drab said. "A fat old man named Slaughter."

The stranger shook his head, and it looked as though his neck had been broken and badly fixed. "That is not the man I am looking for. Are you sure that he was a fat old man?"

"Oh, yes, sir. We saw him finished off on this very spot," Officer Dross insisted.

The stranger stamped a foot. I could have sworn that he had claws for feet, but his feathery leggings half covered them. "Maybe he was in disguise," he creaked.

Officer Dross looked at Officer Drab. "You *did* say that his face looked painted when you cut him down, Officer Drab."

"I *did*," Officer Drab agreed. "Some of it came off on my hands! Here, look!"

"Ugh!" Officer Dross cried. "You mean to say that you served my breakfast with those hands? You didn't *wash* them first?"

"You were never bothered before," Officer Drab told him.

"Officers!" the stranger cawed. "Just tell me. What did they do with the body?"

Officer Drab and Officer Dross said, "Took it to the Storm Inn."

"And where will I find this inn?"

"By the riverside," Officer Drab told him and began to explain how to get there. I turned and ran. I didn't know Eden City very well, but I knew it well enough to get to the inn by the side streets and alleys. Maybe I could get there before the Avenger . . . because I had no doubt that's who the hideous creature was.

Maybe I could warn Theus that the Fury was on its way.

What I didn't know was that Theus had already collected his wings and left . . .

★★★

Theus had the wings tucked under one arm and his ancient Greek tunic under the other. He looked up into the skies for the Fury and was ready to flee. He didn't know that the bird would go straight to the place where he had died. Only Zeus could go to the

226

place where Theus was *now*.[50]

The Titan reached the corner of the alley where the sign read: "To the Temple of the Hero." In the dull morning light he could see better than he had the night before. The temple was a shabby little building—neglected and crumbling. It was supposed to look like a Greek temple, but it had been made from wood.

What caught Theus's eye was the horse that stood beside the warped door of the temple. There were lots of horses in Eden City. This was the only one with wings. "Pegasus?" Theus laughed. "What are you doing here, boy?" he asked and patted the muzzle of his old friend.

The door to the temple scraped open, hanging off its rusted hinges. An old woman came out, dressed in a faded shawl and carrying some dead flowers. Her eyes were not much brighter than the Eden City puddles. She looked up at Theus. "The hero is back," she said. "I've spent all my life waiting for the hero to

---

50   Zeus, of course, was able to track down Theus by the ring on his finger. You were told this in an earlier chapter. Pay attention. I warned you that things would start to get hectic now.

come home, and now he has. I must tell all the other worshippers."

"Wait!" Theus said. "Who is this hero?"

The woman was impatient. "He came to Eden City two hundred years ago. He died, but he saved the city—we set up the temple to remember him. To thank him."

"With sacrifices?" Theus asked.

The woman showed her yellowed teeth in a broken grin. "Don't be silly—with flowers and hymns." She hurried down the alley toward the main street to spread the news, singing one of her hymns:

"Thank you to the greatest ever.
We will forget you never.
Come back someday; come and see us;
We will welcome you back . . ."

And she disappeared around the corner into the bustling street.

Theus stepped through the door of the temple. The inside was a simple room with a table at one end. There were fresh flowers on the table—the ones that the old woman had brought that morning. There were stone statues that looked like Greek gods. But there was a living one on a throne in the middle of the room. "Come in, cousin Theus. You don't have much time," he said.

"Hello, Zeus," Theus said with a smile.

★★★

I ran into the Storm Inn and saw January with a tablecloth. She was wrapping a few clothes and shoes into the cloth. "Jim? What are you doing here?" she asked.

"Looking for Theus," I said. "I wanted to warn him. An enemy of his is in town."

She frowned. "When I got here, he was just leaving. He'd found his wings and was rushing off. I think he must know about this enemy."

"I'm sure he guessed," I said. "Did he fly away?"

She looked at me like I was crazy. "Fly? Theus can't fly. Nobody can fly."

"Of course not," I said quickly. "Where did he go?"

"Said something about the Temple of the Hero."

"He doesn't have time for that," I groaned. "I'd better go and warn him," I said as I turned to go. "See you at the station in half an hour."

I ran out of the swinging doors and turned right. I

ran so quickly that I didn't see the hawk-faced stranger coming down the street from the left. The Avenger was closing in on us fast.

It turned into the Storm Inn and stared at January. [51]

"Good morning, sir. Sorry, but we're not open yet," she told the creature.

"The door is open," it told her.

"The door is broken—along with most of the furniture," she said. "We had a fight in here last night."

"Ah." The beaked head nodded crookedly. "And a young man was killed?"

"No . . . that was Big Bill, the night before. He had a thin skull. It's a shame, really."

"But someone died down the road from here—at dawn—at a place you call the jailhouse?"

January nodded. "An old thief." She didn't trust the stranger and wasn't going to tell him the full truth. "His little boy is a friend of mine."

---

51 I have to believe January about this part of the story. I guess she must have been telling the truth because, by accident, she found the only way in all of the universe to delay the Fury and give Theus a chance. What was this "only way"? Oh, come on! I know you're not a writer, but you must have figured it out. No? Then you'll just have to keep reading . . .

"And where is this little boy now?" the stranger asked.

"Just ran along to the Temple of the Hero."

"Ahhh! Perhaps I should ask *him* if he knows about this death at the jailhouse?" the bird said and turned to go. If I had left then, he'd have caught me at the temple *and* caught Theus. Only one thing could stop him . . .

January knotted the cloth and patted the bundle. The town hall clock struck 9:30. "Just enough time for a bite to eat before I leave," she said.

"Ah," the Fury sighed as it reached the door. "I haven't eaten for two days. My usual supply escaped . . ."

"Two days? You must be starving. You could share mine. I have a big pot of stew in the kitchen. My father won't have many customers in here tonight. It will just rot and go to waste."

"No, thank you," the Fury said. "I must get along to this temple." It stretched out a feathered arm to open the door.

"All right then," January said brightly. "But it's a shame. It's my favorite." The monstrous bird was almost out of earshot when January said the magical word that may have saved Theus. "It's liver," she said.

The Fury stopped. Saliva dripped from its cruel beak. It sighed. "Ohhhh! Why didn't you say so? In that case, I will have some, young lady."

"You want a bowl full?"

"No, just bring me the whole pot!"

And that was how the Fury wasted a precious ten minutes, while I stood inside the Temple of the Hero . . .

TWENTY-NINE

I don't know about you, but I would like to pause for a chapter break. My heart races when I remember the events of that morning. My heart was racing then, too—but at the time I didn't know exactly how close we were to disaster. Imagine—one little word like "liver" made all the difference!

I had been here before. Standing in the shadows and watching the Titan Prometheus talking to Zeus the god. The first time had been in Mr. Mucklethrift's library. That time, the city had shivered and stayed silent. Now it listened, like a blackbird waiting by a wormhole for the sound of a wiggle.

Just as before, Zeus and Theus seemed to know I was there, yet they did not seem to care.

"You have found the Temple of the Hero," Theus

said. "So there *is* a human hero—the gods can forgive me now?"

"No, Theus—just because this hero has a temple doesn't mean that he really is a hero. You need to find him and show him to me."

Theus nodded. "I'll have to travel back two hundred years or more."

Zeus leaned forward on the throne. "That may be a wise trip to make. I can forgive you . . . but I cannot call off the Fury. The Avenger will hunt you to the ends of the universe."

"So what's the use of finding a hero?" Theus cried.

"Cousin," the god said. "I cannot help *you*. But I can help the *humans*."

Theus jumped forward. "You can clear the world of all this foul air? Stop them from living in smoke and fog?"

"No!" Zeus thundered. "THAT is your fault. THAT is what happened because YOU gave them fire. The humans will have to learn their own lessons about how to use fire wisely."

"I could teach them," Theus said.

"Not while you are fleeing from the Fury, you

couldn't," Zeus said and settled back a little. "I have been into the future, Theus—one hundred and fifty years from now. This smoke will make the world too warm. The ice peaks will begin to melt, and the seas will rise to flood Earth. The deserts will spread to swallow up the fields. THEN the humans will learn their lesson. Wisdom comes from making mistakes—not from listening to preachers and teachers."

"Will they learn too late?"

Zeus shrugged. "I haven't been any farther into the future, Theus. No, I cannot stop their insanity with their use of fire. But you have acted bravely—like a true Greek hero. You gave your life for the old man even though it meant that you gave off a green spark, betraying you to the Fury."

"He's here?" Theus asked, and for the first time I saw him tremble.

"He's near," Zeus warned. "You have shown so much care for these humans that I will do something for them. It will be your reward. I will take away some of Pandora's terrors from this brutal city. I will make it a better place to live."

"How will you do that?" Theus asked.

"I'll think of something, Theus. Leave it to me. The humans of these days have forgotten us great Greek gods. But we still have our powers. We are as old as Earth and twice as tired—but maybe there are some small things that we can still do before we sail beyond the sunset. One last noble deed. I'll think of something."

His godly ears picked up some small sound that my human ears must have missed—or maybe his godly nose scented it. He stood up quickly and pushed Theus toward the door of the temple. "It's time that you were flying."

Pegasus gave a soft warning whinny. It stood in the courtyard outside the door. We all looked through the opening. At the far end of the alley stood the hooked and feathered fiend, searching and sniffing the air for its prey.

Theus threw on the swan wings and ran to the door with a leap, and in a beat of the wings he was off the ground. The Fury saw him and began to scramble down the alley, but the path between the high houses was too narrow for it to spread its wings and too slick with mud for it to run.

I couldn't stop the Fury. But I could slow it down.

I ran to Pegasus and gave it a kick, much harder than I'd ever kicked Uncle's coffin. The startled horse cried and spread its wings. It leaped into the air just as the Fury reached the courtyard and flapped into the air. The two collided over the rooftops. Their wings tangled, and they tumbled back down into the muddy alley.

Sadly for the Avenger, the horse landed on top of it. Pegasus rolled clear and shook itself free. But the Fury just lay there and groaned. "You've broken my neck—again," it hissed.

I looked up to the clouds and cried, "Good luck, Theus . . . and thanks!"

Zeus laughed. Eden City's shadows sighed as their victim flew free from their claws.

The town hall clock struck a quarter to ten, and I knew I had to run to reach the train—the train that would carry me and Uncle Edward into a new future.

I raced through the tangled streets. I passed the dying match girl and turned into an alley that I was sure was a shortcut. It led to a high fence and a dead end.

I raced back, slithering in puddles, hurrying past the jail. I'd forgotten which way to go. I looked around wildly. I turned right. My lungs were burning with the effort. I turned right again . . . and almost tripped over the legs of the match girl. I'd gone in a circle.

The savage city was playing cat and mouse with me again. The snickers in the shadows were louder now— more like loud laughs and shrieks of joy. But when I stopped to listen, there was a silence as soft as the movement of a fly on a spider's web.

That was it! It wasn't cat and mouse any longer. I was a fly caught up in Eden City's spiderweb of streets. The more I struggled, the more trapped I became. It was like a bad dream. I felt a tug on my jacket. The match girl looked up at me with skin as pale and frail as paper.

"Turn left, then right, left, then right again," she said in a voice no more than a whisper.

"Thanks," I said, sobbing. But she didn't hear. She slumped back against the wooden wall of the corner store.

"Thanks," I said again and raced off the way that she had told me.

The clock began to chime the hour. I saw the station entrance across the road. "Come on!" Eden

City was taunting. "Come on! You can make it if you *really* try!"

But it was a trick to tempt me toward a flat finish. I leaped off the sidewalk. A carriage horse brushed against me, knocking me back into the gutter. It saved me from being crushed under the wheels.

The shadows snickered.

Tick! the time ticked. *Dong!* the hour began to chime. The crossing sweeper helped me get to my feet. I scrambled across the road, too short of breath to even breathe a "thanks."

January was waiting by the steaming train as I rushed onto the platform. Porters loaded our coffin into the front carriage. Uncle Edward would be free as soon as we were out of this bleak place.

We stepped onto the train, and it began to move.

"Theus got away," I panted. "He should be all right." I closed my eyes and felt the sweat trickle into them.

Then I felt a rough handkerchief wipe the sweat away. When I opened my eyes, January was smiling at me. She wasn't so ugly when she smiled.

The shadows of Eden City sighed. They knew that they'd been defeated.

January kissed me. Her lips tasted faintly of liver.

"We're all going to be all right," she said with a smile.

EPILOGUE

EDEN CITY—1863

You'll have gathered that I wrote this story years after it happened. Sometimes that amazing year of 1858 seems like a dream within a dream. But look at the history books, and you will see that Eden City began to change that year. When I left, it was a place with all of the sorrows of Pandora's curse. When I returned, it wasn't a new Olympus—but it had been touched by the gods. That's how I knew that my two days with Prometheus hadn't been a dream. So let me take you back, just five years on . . .

January and I stepped off the train and looked around Eden City station. "We got off at the wrong stop," January said.

It seemed so different from the Eden City that

we'd left five years before. The people who bustled around the platforms seemed so . . . *cheerful*! The shadows no longer sucked at your soul and snickered. Now they seemed to smile.

Uncle Edward stepped down after us—a little fatter and with his hair dyed brown. After all, Uncle Edward was supposed to have been hanged here five years earlier. We called him Uncle Edwin now . . . dead Edward's twin brother.

Jan had changed the way we lived. She told us that we were such good actors that we could make a good living from doing our shows—we didn't need to rob the rich and risk the rope in every town that we visited. And Jan turned out to have a talent for acting, too. We added new plays for her to perform in. We borrowed some of the gentleman writer's tales—Jan's "Death of Little Belle" made grown men weep.[52]

We were invited everywhere and paid enough to let us live well.

---

52 Of course, I still loved doing "The Uncle" with Skinny the skeleton, and "The Boy Stood on the Burning Deck" had audiences jumping to their feet to applaud. January was good—but not as good as me. Sorry . . . she has read this and says that I am dreaming. She says that she is the best thing to have happened to me and Uncle Edward in our miserable lives. I will never admit that . . . I may agree, but I will never admit it.

Of course, January and I had grown by the time that we returned. My ban from Eden City was over, but I doubted whether any police officers would have recognized the tall, strong young man who stepped off the train as little Jim, the thief.

Jan's own father would not have recognized the red-haired girl in the cotton dress who stood next to me.

"It LOOKS like Eden City," I said. "But it's . . . changed."

A girl with rosy cheeks and golden hair stepped toward us with an arm full of flowers. "Welcome to Eden City," she said. She gave January a handful of flowers, smiled, and said, "Enjoy your stay."

Jan shook her head. "Thank you . . . but is this what you do? Give flowers away to travelers?"

The flower girl smiled brightly. "Yes, it's a wonderful job. Five years ago I was living on the streets, selling matches and slowly dying."

"I remember you," I said quietly. "What happened?"

"Mr. Mucklethrift, the good neighbor of Eden City, rescued me from the streets and got his doctors to make me well again."

Uncle Eddie shook his head. "But *why*?" he asked. "He was the meanest, cruelest man I ever met."

"He *was*," she agreed. "Then, they say, he had a dream—a visit from a spirit—and it changed his life. It changed all of our lives. Now he gives all the money from the factory to Eden City to make it a better place. It still has its smoke, I know," she said, "but the people are happy, thanks to Mr. Mucklethrift."

Then I knew that Zeus had kept his promise. He said that he'd reward Theus for his brave deed. He said he'd take away some of Pandora's terrors from this brutal city and make it a better place to live.

What had he done? Later that day we went to Mucklethrift Manor. The streets of Eden City were clean. Officers Drab and Dross were now there to help people. "Not much crime in Eden City," Drab said, smiling. "The last big case we had here was when Mayor Tweed was thrown into jail for stealing the city's taxes."

"You can't drive out all the greed in the world, I guess," Uncle Eddie said.

The policeman agreed. "But the people of Eden City have enough money to get by on. They don't need to steal. The people in the factory are well paid, and Mr. Mucklethrift built a special place for the city's orphan babies. The baby farm was closed down. Mr. Mucklethrift even makes sure that the poor and the street beggars are well cared for at the Storm Inn."

"The Storm Inn?" January said. "What a strange place to care for the poor!"

"No! It's a shelter for the needy now," the policeman explained. "Mr. Storm serves such good food!"

"He *does*?" Jan gasped. "He must have been taking cooking lessons."

"The food is so good that even the rich go there to taste his stew—they travel from miles around to savor his special dish."

"Liver?" I asked.

"How did you guess?"

"Just a hunch," I said.

"Enjoy your stay," Drab said. We walked on down the street, and he called after us, "Oh . . . and I am sorry about what happened to your brother, Mr. Slaughter," he said.

"We got over that," Uncle Eddie said with a smile.

At the Mucklethrift factory gates workers strolled outside to chat and enjoy their coffee break. A notice on the gate read: "Sorry, we do not employ children under the age of twelve." The chimneys still poured their purple and yellow smoke into the dead air. But Zeus had said that he could not stop the humans' insanity with their use of fire.

The clean streets and the brightly painted shops saw little of the weak autumn sun through the smog. Still, Eden City was a better place than the one we had left. Only the tumbledown Temple of the Hero looked as derelict as it had been before.

The front door of Mucklethrift Manor was open when we arrived, and a smiling butler welcomed messengers, businesspeople, and visitors. "Of course Mr. Mucklethrift will be happy to see you. He still talks about the show that your brother did five years ago, Mr. Slaughter. It was the very next day that he had the visit from the spirit, you know?"

"Ah, and that visit changed him, did it?"

"Indeed. Your dead brother changed Eden City forever."

"He did?" Uncle Eddie blinked.

"Go into the library. Mr. Mucklethrift will be pleased to see you."

And the old man was. He shook hands with us

warmly and sat us down at the library table—the one where Zeus and Theus had met those five long years before. His tale was a strange one. Only Jan and I really understood what had happened.

"We hanged your brother," Mr. Mucklethrift said. "Mayor Tweed insisted. But I was never happy about it. And that night, when I fell asleep, he visited me."

"Mayor Tweed visited you in bed?" Uncle Eddie exclaimed.

"No. No! No! Your dead brother's spirit visited me. I woke as the town hall clock struck one and saw him standing at the foot of my bed. I was afraid."

"I would be too," January agreed.

"He said I was too greedy and didn't care about my fellow humans. Then he set up his old magic lantern and showed me pictures. But the pictures were moving, talking pictures, not like your usual magic lantern."[53]

53 Moving, talking pictures are impossible, of course. Mr. Mucklethrift should have guessed that this wasn't the spirit of Uncle Eddie. Maybe he was so scared that he believed everything he saw. But you're not scared. YOU know that this was Zeus in the form of Uncle Eddie.

"And what did you see?" Uncle Eddie asked.

"Ah, I saw the horrors of Eden City. The suffering of the baby farm and the begging. And, worst of all, a dying match girl in the gutter."

"Horrible," Uncle Eddie agreed.

"Then he showed me my own future. He showed me moving pictures of a place he called the underworld. There was a dog with three heads—it would let me into the underworld but would tear me apart if I ever tried to get out."

"Cerberus," Uncle Eddie said. He knew a lot about old tales.

"The tortures in that underworld were too horrible to repeat," Mr. Mucklethrift said. "I tried to tell your brother's ghost that he was just a nightmare. But he opened the door, and in walked the most hideous creature that I have ever seen . . . or smelled! It had three heads—heads that squabbled with each other—but when they worked together, they could breathe huge puffs of fire that would burn me into ashes!"

Then I knew that Zeus had brought his palace pet, the Chimera, to Eden City. That would be monster enough to frighten *any* man out of his misery.

Mr. Mucklethrift's eyes widened. "The lion head kept roaring at the goat head. It was scary. And Mr. Slaughter's spirit said something about 'escaping from the power of Pandora.' What do you think he meant?"

"He meant that you must do your best to drive misery out of Eden City," I said. "That would be the only way to escape your fate."

He nodded. "That's what I thought. And that's what I've tried to do ever since. I sold most of my riches to make Eden City a better place for us all to live in. And the money from my factory keeps it that way. Do you think Edward Slaughter has forgiven me for having him hanged?"

"Has he been back since that night?" Jan asked.

"No. I never saw him."

"Then Edward Slaughter is resting," she said.

Uncle Eddie smiled. "Edward Slaughter forgives you."

★★★

And that, dear reader, only leaves poor Prometheus. I cannot tell you where he is or whether he has escaped the Avenger.

I would like to think that he has.

When he took off from the Temple of the Hero, the damaged Avenger set off after him. I think that the Avenger flew into the future. If I'd have been the Fury, that's what I would have done.

But I know that Prometheus was still looking for the hero. There was only one place to find him—somewhere in the gloomy, grimy past of Eden City. If Theus is in the past and the Fury is in the future, then Theus is safe.

The Titans and the gods and we hairless human creatures are all made from the same stuff . . . from the dust of distant stars. So Theus and Zeus, January and I, are all cousins.

And so are you, dear reader.

I wonder if Theus will ever find that hero?

I hope so. That's the one thing Pandora left us—hope.

GLOSSARY

The Avenger/The Fury: An eagle with god-given powers, it was commanded by Zeus to rip out Prometheus's liver every day.

Cerberus: The three-headed watchdog who guarded the entrance to the underworld. A child of the giant Typhon and Echidna, Cerberus permitted new spirits to enter the realm of dead but allowed none of them to leave.

The Chimera: A monster who breathed raging fire. It had three heads—one of a lion, another of a goat, and another of a serpent. Its front was a lion, its middle a dragon, and its back part a goat.

Hades: The lord of the dead and ruler of the underworld. When the three sons of Cronus divided the world among themselves, Hades was given the underworld, while his brothers, Zeus and Poseidon, took the "upper world" and the sea respectively.

Hephaestus: The son of Zeus and Hera, he was the god of fire and craftsmanship.

Hera: The queen of the Olympian deities. She was a daughter of Cronus and Rhea and the wife and sister of Zeus. Hera was mostly worshipped as a goddess of marriage and birth.

Hercules: The son of the god Zeus and Alcmene. His gift was his amazing physical strength. His main adversary was Hera—she eventually drove him insane.

Hermes: The son of Zeus and also the messenger of the gods. It was his duty to guide the souls of the dead to the underworld.

Pandora: The first woman on Earth. Zeus ordered Hephaestus, the god of craftsmanship, to create her, and he did, using water and soil. Pandora had a jar that she was told not to open under any circumstances. Too curious, Pandora opened the jar, and all evil escaped and spread over the world. She closed the lid when the entire contents of the jar had escaped, except for one thing that lay at the bottom—and that was hope.

Pegasus: The winged horse that was fathered by Poseidon with Medusa.

Prometheus: A Titan who stole fire from Zeus and the gods. In punishment, Zeus commanded that Prometheus be chained for eternity to the Caucasus Mountains. There, an eagle would eat his liver, and each day the liver would regrow again, making the punishment endless.

Zeus: The youngest son of Cronus and Rhea, he was the supreme ruler of Mount Olympus and of the pantheon of gods who resided there. He upheld the law, justice, and morals and was the spiritual leader of both gods and humans.

GREECE—AROUND 4,000 YEARS AGO

I wasn't there myself, but I met someone who knows exactly what went on in those days. You will have to trust me when I tell you that every word of this story is true . . . probably. All right, a LOT of it is true. Other parts I may have made up to fill in the gaps so that it all makes sense. Yes, you'll see that I tell a lot of lies. But liars are the only people you CAN trust in this world.

Zeus sat on a cloud.

You can do that sort of thing when you're a Greek god. But YOU shouldn't try it. You would need a very long ladder to get up to the clouds, and as soon as you stepped off, you would probably fall clean through the cloud. This could get very messy—especially if someone is walking underneath you.

Only special people like me and my pa could sail up and over the clouds. How could I do that? Wait and see.

Where was I? Oh, yes, Zeus on his cloud. He wore wings and was the most beautiful thing you've ever

i

seen—so beautiful that ordinary people (like you and me) couldn't bear to look at him.[1]

Next to Zeus sat his wife, Hera, and she was not so beautiful because she had a scowl on her face. Her nose crinkled like a caterpillar's back, and her lips were as thin as an ant's leg.

"You promised me a vacation," she snapped.

"This is a vacation, dearest," Zeus said and smiled. "A sparkling blue sea and miles of sandy beach."

"The beach is covered with human corpses!" she screeched.

"There's a war on, my lovely," her husband said with a shrug. "We can sit and watch it just as those humans watch their little plays at the theater."

Hera pouted. "I wouldn't know. You never take me to the theater."

"This is real life—much more fun," he argued. "We can even join in."

"You are too mean to take me to the theater. You're so mean that you'd steal a dead fly from a

---

1 "Aha!" you cry. "Last week I was starving, and a cheese sandwich was the most beautiful thing I'd ever seen! More beautiful than a Greek god." All I can say is this: if you keep crying out like that, I'll never get on with my story. So stop arguing and listen.

blind spider."

"Only if you were feeling hungry," he muttered.

Hera didn't hear. Just as well.

"The town stinks," she said. "Humans stink. I don't know why you don't just send down a thunderbolt and burn it to the ground. A good fire would clean it up."

"Ah, fire," Zeus said and nodded. "They don't need my fire. The humans can make fire for themselves."

Hera turned to him with a face as sharp as a shrew. "And who *gave* them the power of fire?"

"I know," Zeus said and sighed.

Hera slapped and plumped up the cloud to make herself more comfortable. "I asked you a question, Zeus. Who gave them fire?"

"My cousin Prometheus," Zeus said and closed his eyes. He was wishing that he hadn't mentioned it.

"Yes, your cousin Theus! He stole fire from the gods and gave it to those creeping little, fighting little, *stinking* little humans."

"Don't get on my back. I have punished him . . ." Zeus began.

"Oh, you *punished* him. You had him chained to a rock. And every day the Avenger came down in the shape of an eagle and ripped out his liver. What sort of punishment is that?" Hera snapped, and thundery sparks crackled in the cloud.

"Every night the liver grew back, so he had to suffer the agony every day for two hundred years . . ." Zeus argued and grew angry as the cloud grew dark.

"But what happened? Eh? What happened?" Hera sneered. "You let him escape!"

"I didn't exactly *let* him . . ."

"All right. You let Hercules *rescue* him. Same difference. And where is Theus now? Hiding. He's traveled through time and space, and he could be anywhere. The poor little Avenger has worn out its wings looking for him!"

"*Poor*? *Little*? It's a blooming great bird with the sharpest beak this side of Mount Olympus. Its talons can rip a rhino's skin . . ."

"Don't argue with me, Zeus. You always lose," Hera said with a shake of her head. "Theus gave fire to the humans, and he got away with it. I only hope that the Avenger finds him one day. It's still out there searching!"

Zeus propped himself up on an elbow. "I *did* make Theus a promise, my dear. I gave him a challenge. I said that if he could find one true human hero, I'd forgive him!"

Hera snorted . . . and then her nose twitched as the stench from the city slipped into her nostrils. "He'll fail. He'll never find a human hero. The Avenger will find Theus first."

"The Avenger will be a bit busy, my dear," Zeus said and peered over the edge of the cloud to the city by the sea below. "There will be a lot of warriors here who need to be taken down to Hades and the underworld. I'm tired of this Troy."

"You're like a baby," Hera said and laughed bitterly. "You soon get tired of a new toy."

"I said *Troy*, not *toy*," Zeus said with a sniff. "The Greeks have been trying to take the city for *ten years* now—*that's* not getting tired *quickly*! Ten *years*!"

Hera rolled over and lay on her stomach next to her husband. The gods gazed down.

Inside the city the ragged Trojans trudged through the streets, thin and weary from the endless war. With secret tunnels and hidden doors, enough food had slipped into the city to keep them going for ten years. Bottomless wells of sweet water would last them forever. But the spirit of the people was as threadbare as their clothes. They longed for freedom. Freedom from a city that had become a prison—

freedom from the fear that their prison walls would fall and let in sharp, slicing, stabbing death.

There were no rats in the city of Troy. They'd all been eaten long ago.

Outside the city a thousand Greek ships rested and rotted on the hot shore. Tattered tents stood, faded and patched, flapping in the warm wind that blew over the soft sand. Slouching soldiers sat on rocks, polished their worn weapons for the 3,600th time, and longed for home.

"So, what are you going to do about it, husband?" Hera asked.

"Put an end to it," Zeus said.

Hera nodded. "And would you like me to tell you who is going to win?"

Zeus's shoulders dropped. "You are going to anyway."

Hera gave a small smile like a cat that's cornered a bowl of milk. "The Greeks are going to enter Troy. They are going to kill the pathetic Prince Paris and his hideous Helen."

"I thought you might say that," Zeus muttered. Hera held a big grudge against Paris and Helen. Ten years ago the goddesses held a beauty contest, and Prince Paris was the judge. Hera offered the judge power over all of

Asia. Athena, the goddess of war, offered him victory wherever he fought. Aphrodite, the goddess of love, offered him the gift of the most beautiful woman in the world. And everyone knew that was Helen of Sparta.

Paris chose Aphrodite as the winner and won the hand of Helen. Hera chose to sulk.

"I hate Helen! Hate her, *hate* her, HATE HER!" she cried.

"You don't like her, then?" Zeus said with a smile.

"I can't TELL you how much I hate her," she screamed, and the cloud shivered and shook out a storm of raindrops onto the dusty heads of the Trojans below. "She is *not* the most beautiful woman in the world—her hair is too straight, her nose is too short, and as for her ears . . . well, what can I say about a woman with ears like that?"

"And she's married to Menelaus, of course," Zeus added, stoking up his wife's rage.

"Ooooh! Yes! A faithless woman. Married to poor King Menelaus, and still she ran off with Paris of Troy." Hera pulled back her lips in a savage sneer. "Her Troy boy!" she said and looked pleased with her little joke. "And just look at the trouble she's caused," she added with a sweep of her hand at the scene below. "A thousand ships and fifty thousand soldiers sent to take her back to Greece. Me? I'd leave her to rot in Troy. From the smell of the place, it is rotting already."

Zeus sniffed and nodded.

Hera turned quickly to Zeus. "So? Whose side are you going to join? If you let *Troy* win, then I will make you wish that you lived in Hades with all of the tortures that the humans suffer there after death."

Zeus held up his mighty hands. "Oh, don't worry, wife. Troy will *lose* because the old curse says that Paris will bring about the destruction of the city. We can't go against the old curses," Zeus said.

"The old curse also says that the Greek hero Achilles will die in Troy." She jabbed a finger at the Greek tents on the plains of Troy. "He's still alive."[2]

Zeus rubbed his eyes tiredly. "Yes, there's so much to do. I don't know where to start."

"Send for the Avenger," Hera told him. "It'll be handy to have it around when Achilles and Paris are

2 Hera and Zeus could SEE Achilles wandering around the camp because they had incredible eyesight. If you could fly, like me, you would see people on the ground like ants. But the gods had eyes like telescopes (binoculars?). Amazing but true.

killed. The Avenger can take them straight to Hades."

Zeus nodded, placed his fingers on his lips, and gave a whistle that shook the walls of Troy. It also made Hera's ears ring.

"Must you?"

"I have to send for Hermes, our messenger."

"Right. *Then* you need to arrange for Achilles to die . . . and *then* you have to make sure that the Greeks get inside Troy and kill Paris."

Zeus nodded slowly. "Yes, that's what I need to do," he agreed.

Hera puffed out her cheeks and blew with pride—which caused a sandstorm on the beach and tattered the tents again. "Phooey! I honestly don't know *what* you'd do without me, Zeus," she said.

"I'd like a chance to find out," he muttered under his breath.

"What was that?"

"I said, dear, I think you've blown some fires out!"

"Fires out? What are you talking about, Zeus?"

"Nothing, dear," the great god said and then turned as he heard a fluttering of wings. A young man landed on the cloud, wearing a bag at his waist. He held a wooden rod with snakes twined around it.

There were wings on his sandals and wings on his helmet and a spoiled look on his face. "Ah, here's Hermes," Zeus said.

"What do you want this time, my foul stepfather?" Hermes said with a sigh.

Zeus took a deep breath and held his temper. It wasn't easy.

"I want you to find the Avenger and bring it to Troy."

Hermes threw down his rod, and the shocked snakes hissed in their surprise. "Ooh! He wants me to find the Avenger. Just like that? I say, just like that?"

Zeus punched the cloud in anger . . . but punching clouds doesn't do you much good. He began to speak quickly in a low, angry voice. "Hermes, you are the messenger of the gods, and it is your job to take messages. So will you please stop complaining about it and get on with what you are paid to do?"

Hermes blinked. "Paid? When have you ever *paid* me? I am rushed off my winged feet, morning to night and night to morning. And not *only* do I not get paid, but I don't even get any *thanks*. All I get is shouted at!" He pulled at the hem of his tunic and blew his nose on it.

"You've made Hermes cry now," Hera groaned. "Say you're sorry, Zeus."

"You're sorry, Zeus," the god growled and then turned back to the sniffling messenger. "Hermes. *Please* do this small thing for me, and I will be so very grateful that I will never shout at you again."

"Promise?" Hermes said and sniffed.

"Promise," Zeus said. "The Avenger is traveling through time looking for Cousin Theus. Theus and the Avenger were last seen in a place called Eden City in a time the humans call 1858."

"Time? I have to travel through time?" Hermes screeched.

"We'll be *so-o* very grateful," Hera told him. "We'll have a special party for you when you get back."

Hermes's face lit up. "A party? With cupcakes?"

"Yes, dear," Hera said. She picked up the hissing rod and handed it to him. "Now, off you go, through time. Tell the Avenger that we're in Troy."

As Hermes's wings began to beat like a hummingbird, Zeus waved. "Have a nice *time!*"

Hera rubbed her hands together. "That's that problem solved. Now . . . *how* are you going to kill

Achilles?" she asked.

Zeus smirked. "I have a rather neat little plan, my dear. A brilliant plan, a work of a genius, even if I do say so myself."

"Hmm!" Hera said. "We'll see."

★★★

Somewhere, just beyond the farthest star, the Greek demigod Prometheus drifted on white wings.

It was lonely out there. He headed for home.

ABOUT THE AUTHOR

Terry Deary writes both fiction and nonfiction. His books have been translated into 28 languages. Terry's *Horrible Histories* series has sold 20 million copies worldwide. Terry has won numerous awards, including Blue Peter's Best Nonfiction Author of the Century in the U.K.

Rumors
of Another World

Also by Philip Yancey
in Large Print:

What's So Amazing About Grace?
The Bible Jesus Read

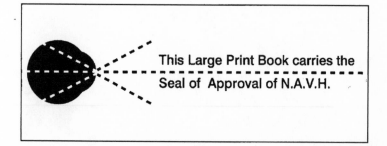

This Large Print Book carries the
Seal of Approval of N.A.V.H.